The Jerk in 7C

DL GALLIE

Published by DL Gallie Author

First published 31st May 2021 as part of Sexy AF

Extended edition published 1 October 2023

Cover designed by **Kristy**, Vanilla Lilly Designs

Special edition designed by **Amanda Walker**, Amanda Walker Design & PA

Edited by **Karen Hrdlicka**, Barren Acres Editing

Proofread by **Margaret Neal**

Formatting and interior design by **DL Gallie**

ALSO BY DL GALLIE

STAND ALONES

Antecedent

Doc Steel

Oops

Off the Books

Fractured:A driven world novel

Deck...the Balls

Secrets and Sunrises

Always in the Cards

Out of Nowhere

Before the Ashes

After the Ashes

Love Me Like You Do

Never Let Me Go

Seven Nights

Seven Kisses

PUCKING NOVELS

I Pucking Hate That I Love You

A Pucking Good Christmas

...and a few pucking more

FALLING NOVELS

These men make it hard not to fall for them

Falling for Dr. Kelly

Falling for Dr. Knight

Falling for Agent Cox

Falling for Agent Cruz

Falling: The Complete Collection

LORDS OF CRESTWOOD PREP

Co-write with Tara Lee

Thatcher

Reign

Hendrix

Saint

THE UNEXPECTED SERIES

When it comes to love, expect the unexpected

The Unexpected Gift

The Unexpected Letter

The Unexpected Package

The Unexpected Connection

The Unexpected series: The Complete Collection

THE CASTAWAY GROVE COLLECTION

Love has arrived in the Grove

Oasis

Unequivocal Love

Five Words

Broken Rules

...and a few more to come.

The Castaway Grove Collection, Vol 1

THE LIQUOR CABINET SERIES

Liquor has never been so disturbingly saucy

Malt Me (Book 1)

Tequila Healing (Book 2)

Wine Not (Book 3)

The Final Shot (Book 4)

The Liquor Cabinet: Series boxset

All of these books are available on Amazon.

They say opposites attract. And we couldn't be any more different.

He's whiskey and ink, and I'm cupcakes and old books.

But our connection is instant. He sets my heart aflutter and my body on fire with just one look.

Until I realize he's the arrogant jerk in 7C.

Suddenly, all that I found appealing becomes a turn-off. The harder I try to ignore him, the more persistent he becomes.

I'm not interested but he's making it clear, he's very interested and will stop at nothing to prove it.

Will we go down together in a blaze of passion or burning hatred?

One way or another, we will set this floor on fire.

To Margaret,

Thank you for all that you do.

Grayson is yours ... his story is coming ... soon ... ish

PROLOGUE
SAXON

...Age 13

"Mom, Dad," I shout, running through the house toward my parents, who are sitting in the great room, or as me and my friends dub it, the 'stick up their ass we have shit taste' room. This room is over-the-top and totally a waste of space. It's decorated in gold, gold, and more gold with brass accents. Deep burgundy drapes with, you guessed it, gold trim. Gaudy paintings line the walls. A fireplace sits front and center in the room, who needs a fireplace when we live in Los Angeles? Sanford and Judy Nobel, that's who. In front of the fireplace is an uncomfortable sofa and to the side are Mom and Dad's throne chairs. They are large, expensive—no surprises there—and an eyesore—the throne chair from *Game of Thrones* is nicer looking than these. Mom and Dad think this room looks elegant but it's far from regal, it looks like gold threw up.

Entering the room, Mom and Dad are sitting on their thrones as if they're royalty. FYI, they're not.

"Saxon, what have I told you about running inside?" Mom scolds me as I come to a stop next to her. Panting from running, I lift my shirt up and wipe my face. Mom hates when I do this but I'm always doing things I shouldn't. Taunting and disappointing my parents is a fun pastime activity for me. When they're berating or yelling, it's the only time I get any attention from them. I'm the black sheep of the Nobels and that stems from my conception. You see, I was an accident. I wasn't in the plan for Judy and Sanford Nobel. They were happy and content with Soraya and Sebastian, my sister and brother. Those two are wanted and loved. They adhere to the vision Mom and Dad have in mind for them. Me? I'm unwanted. Not loved and don't stick to the vision set out for me.

"Sorry, Mom," I reply, my voice loud due to the excitement coursing through my veins.

"And we don't shout," she scolds, again. "We aren't animals."

"Sorry, Mom." That seems to be the most common phrase I say to my parents, especially my mom. I sometimes wonder if Dad even knows he has another son. It often feels like I'm nonexistent to him. "Mom, Marshall invited me to the race with him this weekend, Mr. and Mrs. Kerr said it would be okay for me to go with them."

"No," Dad sternly says, "this weekend is the fundraiser, we need you here." Seems he does notice me, only because I'm 'needed' to keep up appearances.

"Needed or wanted?" I snap.

"Does it matter?" Dad says, not an ounce of emotion in his voice. "You will be here."

What Sanford says is final, there's no arguing with him.

I let out a frustrated huff. "Fine," I growl. Turning on my heel, I stomp out of the great room and head upstairs to my bedroom. The only room in the house that has any character. It's my haven and I'm thankful to have it. Flopping onto my bed, I grab my phone and text Marshall.

SAXON

I can't come this weekend. I'm wanted for a fundraiser

MARSHALL

Wanted or needed?

Does it matter? I can't go with you guys.

It won't be the same without out.

I know he's only saying that to placate me, but it's nice to know someone wants and appreciates me. My phone pings again, this time it's Grayson, my other best friend and the guy next door.

GRAYSON

Marsh just told me you can't come.
Bummer.

SAXON

Bummer all right...maybe I should just sneak away like I did last time???

The last time I was forbidden from going away with them, I said, 'Fuck it' and I went anyway. I didn't think they'd notice I wasn't here but I was wrong. So very wrong. Dad was fuming when Mr. and Mrs. Kerr dropped me home on Sunday evening. He threatened to have them arrested for kidnapping and he threatened to send me to military school. I contemplated what I could do to be sent away, how bad is it that I would have preferred military school to my home? Being sent away would have been better than living here.

I apologized profusely to Keri and Ryan but being the awesome people they are, they shrugged it off and said they'd happily kidnap me anytime. I wish my parents were like Marshall's.

GRAYSON

You think Mr. and Mrs. K will let you?

SAXON

They did say anytime but I don't want to do that to them. Dad will have them charged with kidnapping and I can't do that to them.

Just send me pics

Roger that...see you tomorrow at school

Turning on my stereo, "Go Your Own Way" by Fleetwood Mac blares through the speakers. I know it pisses my parents off when I blast my music but I'm not in the mood to be scolded for a second time, so I grab my Beats and place them on my ears. Sitting on the end of my bed, I lie back and stare at the ceiling. The words to this song resonate with me right now, I can't wait 'til I'm old enough to go my own way and live my life how I want. The day I move out and start living life the way I want to, will be the best day of my life.

PROLOGUE
SIMONE

...Age 11

STARING AT THE CASKET BEFORE ME, MY EYES WELL with tears again. It feels like all I've done for the last week is cry. She's gone. My mom is no longer alive. She went out to run an errand and she never came home. Her last days on this Earth were hooked up to a machine that helped her breathe and pump blood around her body. As she was driving home, she had a stroke and as a result her car veered off the road and into a tree. The injuries she sustained in the accident weren't critical but it was already too late for mom. The stroke deprived her brain of oxygen and blood for too long and there was no chance she'd recover.

Watching Dad fall apart, as he told me the love of his life was gone, broke my little heart and in that moment, I decided I wanted to be a doctor. I want to stop others from feeling like we do right now. I want to save people and make the world a better place. I know there was nothing I could have done to save my mom but maybe, I can help save other people.

"How you doing, Baby Girl?" Dad asks me, pulling me into his side.

Shrugging, I look up at him. "I'm going to be a doctor when I grow up. I'm going to save people like Mom so that no one needs to feel like we feel right now."

Dad smiles for the first time in days, and seeing that causes my lips to lift into a smile as well. "I have no doubt that you will, Baby Girl. Dr. Mitchel has a nice ring to it."

For the first time since losing Mom, I feel happy albeit still sad, but my life has a plan now. I'm going to be the best doctor I can be and make my mom proud.

1

SIMONE

It's pitch-black in my room when I'm, once again, awakened by loud music from the new neighbor next door. He's only been living here for two weeks and every night since he moved in, this is how I've been woken at stupid o'clock. Tonight's alarm clock song of choice is "Go Your Own Way" by Fleetwood Mac—*at least the jerk has good taste in music*—I think to myself as I roll over and glance at the clock on my bedside table. I see it's 4 a.m. "Wow, a sleep in," I grumpily mumble.

Sitting up, I shake my head in frustration and sigh.

Like I do each morning, I bang on our adjoining wall. Not that it does me any good, the jerk doesn't turn the volume down...probably because he can't hear my banging due to the rock concert going on in his apartment.

Climbing out of bed, I walk into the kitchen, and turn on my coffee pot. I need a caffeine boost since it's super early. While waiting for my coffee, I head back into my room to take a shower. Walking into the bathroom, I turn on the faucet, letting the water heat up. Stripping off, I tie my locks into a messy bun and step under the spray. The warm water hitting my skin gets the blood pumping and slowly wakes me up. Grabbing my face wash, I scrub away and then move on to my body. Once I'm rinsed, I climb out and wrap a towel around myself.

Wiping away the steam from the mirror, I grin when I realize that my messy bun is on point; it's messy but put together, and will do for the day. Changing into jeans and a black racer-back tank, I walk back into the kitchen and grin when I see the coffee pot full of liquid black gold. Coffee is life. I don't human without caffeine and people are much safer once I've had a cup...or three. Maybe one morning I should visit Mr. Loud-Music-Playing-Asshole before my coffee, and rip him a new one. Yeah, nah, that's not gonna happen. I'm a lover, not a fighter.

With my mug in hand, I walk over to the window seat and I stare out the glass. San Francisco is gorgeous this time of morning. The city is just waking up. The cityscape brightening as the sun rises into the morning sky. I'm so not a morning person, especially at stupid o'clock, but I will have to get used to getting up at this time once I'm a real doctor. I would much prefer a night shift since I'm a night owl.

I'm in my final year of med school at the University of California, San Francisco and I'm hoping to be accepted into the emergency medicine residency program at UCSF. I can't remember a time when I didn't want to be a doctor. Mom's death was my main motivator for it, but I think even if she was still alive, I'd want to be a doctor. Helping people is engrained in me, I get that from my dad, who just so happens to be my biggest cheerleader. He pushes me to be the best I can be and now that I'm no longer at home, I hope he finds love again. He and Mom had an epic love. I was only little when Mom passed, but I remember the two of them dancing together in the kitchen while she was cooking dinner. They were always touching each other. I know Mom would want him to be happy and now that he's free of raising me, I hope he finds happiness and love again.

After finishing coffee number two, I see it's almost seven. I can't handle the music anymore so I grab my things and head to the library so I can study—in peace—before class later this morning.

Slinging my bag over my shoulder, I exit my apartment. Locking my door behind me, I walk toward the elevator and notice the doors starting to close. I yell out, "Hold the elevator," not expecting it to be held. Then a dainty hand slides through the doors and they open up again, allowing me to race over and climb in. "Thanks," I say with a smile to the gorgeous blonde.

Nodding her head in response, I step next to her and watch the numbers count down as we make our way to the ground floor. Before she steps out, she smiles again. "Have a great day," she cheerfully says before exiting the building.

Turning left on Parnassus Avenue, I head toward campus. As I pass Starbucks, the door opens and my senses are overtaken by caffeine. On autopilot, I find myself inside and ordering a venti latte. With my coffee in hand, I continue on to school.

Heading to the library across from campus, I grab a table in the back and text Nadine, my best friend, to tell her where I am.

SIMONE

back left corner…ready and waiting
textbooks and coffee emoji

A few moments later, my phone vibrates across the table.

NADINE

Why the hell are you up so early?

It's 8…that's not early.

Party central again???

Yep…I'm ready to go over there and
give him a piece of my mind

I'd pay to see that Miss "I'm a Lover Not
a Fighter."

middle finger emoji

See you when you get here

GIF of a captain saluting

Pulling up Spotify, I pop on my rose gold Beats and click play on my study playlist. I quietly sing along to the music and focus on my textbook. I lose myself to medicine and I forget all about the arrogant jerk in 7C.

2

"Later, Buttmunch," Soraya sings out, as she exits my apartment. My sister came to visit a few days ago. I haven't seen her in forever because I was living it up on the other side of the world, while she was back here, forging a name for herself in LA's law scene. Luckily for me, my big sister is pretty awesome. I don't know how long she'll be here, but I don't mind. It's nice reconnecting with her after such a long absence and it's also nice having someone in the apartment when I get home from the bar.

Recently, I opened Nobel's Tavern with silent backing from one of my good friends, Grayson Walker. He was only too happy to help me get my venture off the ground and have a no-hands-on role. He's the lead mechanic for our third amigo, Marshall Kerr's race team with Scofield Racing. Marshall is a few years younger than us but the three of us clicked the first time we met. Marshall signed with Scofield early on in his career but a devastating accident in his rookie season nearly ended it all. But he's a persistent bastard and now, nothing stops him. That's one of the reasons the three of us get along so well, we all are headstrong, pigheaded to some, but when we want something, we will stop at nothing to get it.

There's not a story from my childhood that doesn't involve Grayson, and in the later years, Marshall. If it wasn't for them, especially Grayson, I wouldn't have survived growing up. Grayson lived next door so I spent a lot of time over at his place, he lived in a loving home, not a hell hole like I did. I'm the black sheep of the Nobel family, the accident that Mom and Dad never wanted. They had just started, what is now, one of LA's top law firms, Nobel and Hayes—mom's maiden name. My brother, Sebastian, fell in line and is also a lawyer. As is Soraya, but to the disgust of Mom and Dad, she works for Legal Aid and not at the family firm.

And then there's me.

The child who constantly broke the rules and went against the grain. When I finished high school, I jumped on a plane and went to Australia for a gap year. That year turned into three, and then it turned into a few years traveling and working my way through Europe. Doing odd jobs here, there, and everywhere, while partying like it was nineteen ninety-nine. Eventually, I ended up back in Australia working at a local brewery, Malt Me, before deciding it was time to head home and settle down.

When I returned, I found myself in San Francisco. I started working at the Tavern and that eventually, led me to owning said Tavern. When it came up for sale earlier this year, I jumped at the opportunity to snatch it up. To pay homage to the family AND piss the parentals off, I renamed it—Nobel's Tavern.

Turning off the music, I place my Beats on the bedside table and collapse into bed. When I get home after closing, I crank up the tunes, have a beer, and wind down. I generally climb into bed around seven and wake up sometime in the afternoon when my body decides it's had enough sleep. Then, I crawl out of bed, slip my shoes on, and head down to Mugz, the coffee shop located on the ground floor of the building for a much-needed caffeine hit.

Today, sleep eludes me and I toss and turn. Flipping and flopping in my bed like a fish on land. Looking over at the clock, I see it's lunchtime, so I decide to head out and get some food. Stepping out of the elevator, I bump into a blonde, reaching out I steady her, and when my eyes connect with her chocolate orbs, I'm mesmerized. I can't stop staring at her. Her perfume permeates the air, it's floral, sweet, and ohh so sexy. I'm lost to this woman, it isn't until someone clears their throat that I let her go. Immediately I feel her loss. She smiles shyly at me and steps into the waiting elevator.

Turning around, we stare at one another as the doors close. It isn't until a hand waves in front of my face and says, "Earth to Saxon," that I'm snapped back to the present.

Shaking my head, I look over and focus on the person next to me, it's my sister. "Where were you just now?"

"I...I just saw the most beautiful woman ever."

"Aww, thanks for thinking I'm beautiful, little bro," she teases, gently punching my arm in a playful way.

"Well, yes, you are but this woman, Soraya, shit, I think I'm in love and we haven't even spoken."

"Love at first sight is bullshit, Sax, lust yes. Love, nope."

"Okay fine, I'm in lust with her."

"Well, what's her name?"

"No clue. As I said, we never spoke. It was all a visual and visceral thing."

"You sound like a stalker," she teases. "You can tell me all about my future sister-in-law—"

"Don't get ahead of yourself, Sis. She could be a monster with a pretty face."

"When has that ever occurred?" she sasses back, and before I can reply, she links her arm with mine and pulls me toward Mugz. "You can tell me all about the possible monster with a pretty face, or my future SIL over a cup of tea."

"Coffee, always coffee," I retort.

"Tea, always tea," she goads back.

Then together we singsong, "Unless it's Jack, always Jack."

Jack is my big sis's and my go-to drink, I drink it on the rocks and she girlies it up and drinks a Lynchburg Lemonade. We are one and the same but when it comes to hot beverages, we are complete opposites.

We enter Mugz. She grabs us a table and I order our drinks. While I wait, my mind drifts to the hottie from the elevators just now. I haven't seen her around before so she's either just visiting, new to the building, or I just haven't come across her yet since I've only been living here for the last few weeks.

Prior to getting this place, I was bunking in the office at the Tavern. The couch in my office is an uncomfortable piece of shit. As soon as I can afford it, I'm going to upgrade to a black leather sofa.

Our order is called, taking the drinks from the barista I make my way over to Soraya, who's grinning like a loon. "What's got you all giddy?" I say, startling her and she drops her phone...big mistake because on the screen, staring up at me is a dick pic.

"Is that what I think it is?" I ask her, scrunching my face up because no one wants to see a dick pic. From the look on my sister's face, she clearly doesn't mind because her cheeks are flushed and it's not an embarrassed shade of pink, it's a turned on 'I like dick pics' shade of pink.

"If you think it's a dick pic, then yes, you'd be correct."

"Please tell me you didn't send boob or down there pics to the perv?" I point to our nether regions because I don't want to say, or think, about my sister's hooha.

"I'm not that stupid. Mom and Dad would have a conniption if my bits ended up online."

"Good," I say, picking up my drink and taking a sip. "But please enlighten me as to why you are grinning about a dick pic?"

"I'm not grinning." I eye her. "Okay, well yeah, maybe I am grinning, but Ivan and I have been screwing each other for a while. He's not husband material. He's different." She pauses and I just know the next words out of her mouth are going to shock me even more. "He's the mail room guy at work."

"Gives a new meaning to the phrase, junk mail."

She snort-laughs. "Junk mail, good one, dear brother."

Staring at her, I shake my head. This totally isn't what I expected to chat about with my sister today. "You know, mail room guy sounds like a real winner, Sis."

"Shut it, asshole. Between the long hours and the never-ending cases, I don't have time to date. This thing is perfect, when I get an itch, Ivan is the quick fuck that I need. He doesn't want anything serious so it's win/win."

"I didn't need to know that," I tell her.

"You asked," she says with a shrug of her shoulders.

"Yeah, you could have just said it's nothing serious."

"Ohh, okay. Well then, it's nothing serious."

Shaking my head, I laugh. "And I'm the black sheep of the family."

"So because I like dick, that makes me the black sheep now?" she retorts, "You, dear brother, are the one and only sheep of the Nobels. Let me remind you why. A gap year that turned into several. Then when you finally returned, you worked in a bar and now own said bar." She flicks her fingers up as she counts them and when she lays it all out, yeah, I'm totally the black sheep of the family.

"I still did a bar exam...of sorts."

I say this just as Soraya takes a sip of her tea and she proceeds to spit it out. "Oh My God, that's too funny, but do you think next time you tell a joke, you wait 'til I've swallowed?"

"That's what she said," I respond and once again, I end up covered in her sprayed tea. "Seriously, Sis, keep it in your mouth."

"That's what he said," she replies, and the two of us burst out laughing.

"God, I've missed this," I tell her. "How long 'til you head back to LA?"

"On the weekend I have to get back. I have a court appearance first thing Monday morning."

"Well, now that I'm all unpacked, what shall we do?"

"Don't you have to work tonight?"

"I do, but I'm only going to go in to place the orders for the weekend and then I'm all yours."

"You. Me. Jack and pizza."

"Really? We have the most amazing city at our doorstep and you want to hang at home?"

"I don't need to wear a bra at home and if we go out, you'll just find some skank, and I don't need to hear you getting down and dirty while I'm here."

"I don't date skanks."

"I didn't say 'date' I said hook up," she air quotes date, "but you agree your type is skank," she states matter-of-factly.

No, my type is that girl in the elevator, I think to myself. I wonder if I will ever see her again.

3

SIMONE

I MUST BE DREAMING BECAUSE THE MAN I JUST SAW is hotter than hot. When his fingers wrapped around my arm to stop me from falling over, a jolt of electricity like they describe in romance novels sparked through my body. Every nerve ending buzzing and coming alive.

My hands landed on his chest to steady myself and holy hardness, Batman, never have I felt a chest so firm. I imagine underneath his tight, formfitting shirt will be abs of steel and maybe the illusive 'V' leading to his impressive—well, I presume impressive after seeing his hands—dick.

We never said a word to one another but with our eyes and bodies, we had a whole conversation. I've never had a reaction to a man like that before. Stepping into the elevator, I turn around and find him staring intently at me. With our eyes fused to one another, the elevator doors close.

Stumbling backward, my back hits the wall. Lifting my hand to my chest, I rest my palm over my rapidly beating heart as the metal car takes me up to my floor. Stepping out onto level seven, I smile when I'm met with silence. "The arrogant jerk in 7C is out," I murmur to myself as I walk toward my apartment.

Unlocking my door, I enter my apartment and kick off my shoes. Walking barefooted over the hardwood floors, I drop down onto my sofa with my mystery man's face still at the forefront of my mind. His eyes are hazel with flecks of gold and I can still feel his gaze on me. My skin buzzes from his stare and the brief contact.

My phone rings and it snaps my attention back to the present. Standing up, I walk over to my bag and pull it out. I smile when I see it's Dad. "Hey, Daddy-o." I say in greeting.

"How's my baby girl doing?"

"Dad, I'm not a baby anymore."

"You'll always be my baby, even when you're seventy."

"Dad, when I'm seventy, you'll be ninety-seven."

"Spritely and ninety-seven," he jokes. "Now, how are you?"

"Good." Visions of my mystery man once again plague my mind.

“Simone,” Dad shouts.

“What?”

“Where did you go just now?”

“Nowhere,” I tell him, but I immediately know my mistake. I answered too quickly. Gaven Mitchel can read me like a book, even if I’m not in front of him, and currently one hundred fifty plus miles away from him.

“Simone...” he admonishes.

“Fine,” I relent, shaking my head and holding back a grin. “I met a guy today and we had a moment.”

“A moment?” he questions me, not in an interrogating way, in a caring I want to be a part of my daughter’s life way.

“Well, we bumped into each other. He stopped me from falling and we stared at one another as the elevator doors closed.”

“One of thoooose moments,” he teases and then tacks on, “is Dr. Mitchel smitten?”

“I’m not a doctor yet, Dad.”

“But you are smitten?”

Trust Dad to pick up on that. “I don’t know if smitten is the word but I’m definitely...intrigued. Yes, let's go with intrigued.”

“Intrigued is good. Just make sure that my future son-in-law treats you like the angel that you are.”

"Dad, I don't think anyone I choose will be up to your standard."

"As long as you don't date anyone like Dirk the Jerk again, I'll be happy."

"I haven't thought of him in years."

"Good, that little shit for brains doesn't deserve to be thought of."

"Shit for brains, really, Dad?"

"Really, really."

"Dad, I need to get dinner started and then I need to study for an exam tomorrow."

"You've got this, Dr. Mitchel. I have faith in you."

"Thanks, Dad."

After hanging up, I decided to bake. Baking is a go-to activity of mine when I need to relax. I bake brownies and for dinner, I whip up some mac 'n' cheese. With a full tummy and my dessert in hand, I hit the books.

It's only 10 p.m. but I can't keep my eyes open. Changing into my nightie, I climb into bed. I'm so exhausted, I fall asleep before my head hits the pillow.

"It's a Beautiful Day" by U2 blares through the wall, jolting me awake. Jumping out of bed, I bang my fist on the wall, "Some people are trying to sleep, jerk," I shout, but clearly it's falling on deaf ears.

U2 morphs into "Brown-Eyed Girl" by Van Morrison. This dude's music playlist is an emotional freakin' roller coaster but I will give it to him, he has good taste in music. But seriously, does he need to blare it at stupid a.m. every-freakin-day?

Stomping into my en suite, I flick on the light and flinch when I see my reflection. I look like a swamp hag. Looking at my watch, I'm impressed when I see it's 5:30 a.m. "At least it's kinda sorta a reasonable hour today." And then I hear feminine giggles and I shake my head. "He's such a player," I grumble, as I turn on the faucet and climb into the shower.

Emerging ten minutes later, I now look like a semi-decent swamp hag. Grabbing my things, I head down to Mugz to grab a coffee and get some last-minute studying done before my exam today.

Just like yesterday, the blonde and I share the elevator to the ground floor. We both enter the coffee shop. "I need all the coffee today," she whines, a yawn breaking free to emphasize her need for coffee.

"You and me both," I tell her as we walk to the counter together.

We each order our coffees and step to the end counter to wait. "I'm Simone." I say, offering my hand.

"Sor—," she says, just as her phone rings.

"Morning," she cheerily answers. Our coffee orders are called, I grab mine and she grabs her. She mouths goodbye to me and exits the coffee shop, laughing into her phone.

I grab a table in the corner and pull out my textbook. With my cup of liquid gold in hand, I hit the books. I set an alarm because sometimes I get so engrossed in what I'm reading that time passes by and I forget to eat, or miss appointments.

As predicted, I'm so lost in my studies, I jump in fright when the alarm on my phone beeps, alerting me it's time to head to campus. I've been here for two hours already, time flies when you're studying medicine. If I don't know this coursework by now, I never will. Packing away my things, I grab a takeout coffee and head to campus.

Four hours later the exam is over and as I'm walking out of the room, I catch up with Nadine. "How'd you do, Nads?"

"Aced it," she says, and I have no doubt that she did. Nads was BORN to be a doctor. She knows everything and I'm glad to have her on my team. "You?"

"Okay, I think," I reply around a yawn.

"Neighbor have a party again?"

"Yep...thank God for coffee," I tell her, and at the thought of the black liquid gold, my mouth waters. "You wanna meet up later for espresso martinis?"

"We can meet at the Tavern...or Nobels, or whatever the hells it's called now."

"Or we could hit up a cocktail bar and celebrate the fact that we only have two exams left next week."

"I like your style, Dr. Mitchel."

"I'm not a doctor yet, don't jinx it."

"Please, Sim, if anyone in that class is going to make it, it's gonna be you."

"Says Dr. Prescott."

"Exactly, now you need to listen to me. I'm smart and all that shit."

I laugh at her. "You are something else, Nadine Prescott."

"I know. I'll text when I'm in an Uber and on my way to pick you up. Say sevenish?"

"It's a date."

We say our goodbyes and I head home. The smell of coffee hits as the door to Mugz swings open. My mouth waters at the scent coming from inside. I need a little pick-me-up after the early morning and stressful test, so I change course and head toward the coffee shop.

Opening the door, I step inside and hit something hard. Lifting my head, I smile when I see who I just bumped into.

4

SAXON

STEPPING INTO MUGZ, I INHALE AND ENTER A blissful happy state. The scent of the coffee beans immediately invigorates my soul and brings me to life. Someone bumps into me from behind and when I turn around, I smile when I see it's elevator girl.

"Elevator girl," I say.

"Elevator boy," she replies, her lips lifting into a grin, "we bump into each other again."

A laugh escapes me. "Seems so." Feeling brazen, I ask, "Can I buy you a coffee?"

"Sure," she says, "but be warned, I need the biggest, ginormous, most caffeineiest coffee in the history of coffees ."

"Need a boost?"

"A big boost. I was woken up at stupid a.m. by my jerk neighbor and then I had exams all day."

"Sorry to hear that."

"At least I'm sure I aced my exams."

"What are you studying?"

"Medicine."

"So I should be calling you Dr. Elevator Girl then?"

"You could...or you could just call me Simone."

She offers me her hand and like when I grabbed her while she was falling yesterday, a spark ignites between us. "And you can call me just Saxon."

"Nice to meet you, Just Saxon."

When she says my name, I nearly come in my pants. Never has my name sounded so sexy passing through someone's lips. Lips that are plump and totally biteable. Lips I want to feel pressed against mine, or wrapped around my cock.

"What can I get you?" the barista asks us. Garnering my attention and halting my dirty thoughts, away from Simone's delectable lips and my body pressed up against hers. "Coffee," we say at the same time, both of us stepping closer to the counter.

She laughs and it's music to my ears. Never before have I been enamored with a woman like I am with Simone. Even her name is gorgeous.

"Large latte, please," she orders.

"Same for me, thanks." And I quickly hand a twenty over to the cashier.

"You didn't have to do that," Simone says with a smile that lights up her face.

"I did offer to buy you a cup."

"You did, so thank you...the next one is on me."

"You're presumptuous, thinking there will be another coffee date," I tease her.

"Positivity breeds positivity."

"I like that mantra," I tell her, as we find a table and take a seat. "So, Elevator Girl," she eyes me when I use her nickname, "with a positive outlook on life, tell me about yourself."

"There's not much to tell," she offers, brushing a tendril of hair behind her ear. "I'm originally from Chico, California. I'm a med student in my last year at UCSF, and I'm hoping to get into the emergency medicine residency program there. I've just had my interview and now I wait."

"Sounds hard-core," I tell her, I have no clue when it comes to medicine.

"It is. There's only twelve positions and generally over two hundred applicants, so the odds aren't in my favor."

"Wow, that's tough but I'm sure you knocked it out of the park and will be accepted."

"I hope you're right."

"Like that quote from *The Hunger Games,* 'May the odds ever be in your favor' but I'm sure you'll be fine."

"You sound like my dad."

"He sounds like a good man, you should listen to us both."

Our order is called, so I hop up and grab our coffees.

"Here you go," I say, placing her drink in front of her.

"Thanks," she replies. Picking up the mug, she brings it to her lips, but before she takes a sip, she closes her eyes, breathes in deeply, and sighs. Taking a sip, her face morphs into pure joy. Opening her eyes, she catches me staring at her. "What?"

"I've never seen anyone drink coffee like that before."

"Thanks...I think."

"Definitely a compliment, it's like you're in love."

"Hello, it's coffee. Coffee is life and I love life, therefore I love coffee."

"Fair enough. I guess I should try it your way then." Picking mine up, I bring it to my lips, close my eyes, and inhale. My nostrils are assaulted with coffee and a beautiful floral scent. Opening my eyes, I stare across to Simone and take a sip.

"See, coffee is much better when you appreciate it like that."

Nodding my head, I agree...but I think it's more to do with her enticing scent, mixed with the coffee, that makes this the best coffee I have ever had in my life.

"So, Just Saxon," she says, breaking the silence that has fallen between us. "What do you d—" But before she can finish her sentence my phone rings. Glancing at the screen, I see it's Tara, from work.

"Excuse me," I tell her as I stand up and answer. "Hey, Tara, what's up?"

"I need you to come down here, there's an issue with the delivery from the new supplier. The new girl, Dana, is as useless as tits on a bull. Tara O called in sick and I can't get anyone to replace her."

"Don't stress, I'll be there in ten."

"You're a lifesaver," she tells me, relief evident in her voice.

I start walking back to the table. "You do love me," I tease her and we say our goodbyes.

"Sorry, I have to go," I apologize to Simone. I can't read her expression.

"It's fine," she says, "I hope everything is okay."

"It will be. I'll see you round."

"Yep," she replies, letting the 'p' pop. I can hear the disappointment in her voice.

Turning back, I rest my hands on the back of the chair I just exited. "Maybe we can do this again sometime?"

"I'd like that. I'm here quite often so maybe I'll see you around, Just Saxon."

"I look forward to it, Elevator Girl." Throwing her a wink, I turn and head out.

Before I step out onto the street, I look back and see her fanning herself. She looks flushed, she clearly feels what I feel. I thought she was gorgeous yesterday when we bumped into each other but today, actually talking to her, she's the complete fucking package.

I hope we meet again so we can see if there's anything there, apart from the instant attraction.

5

SIMONE

He stands up and takes the call. My eyes follow him as he steps away. I take the moment to check him out and he's hotter than I remember. His eyes are even dreamier and his voice, I could listen to him read the phone book.

When he tells me he has to go, I deflate. I was enjoying getting to know him. He doesn't ask for my number, which kinda sucks, but we have literally only spoken for maybe ten minutes.

I watch him walk away and I unabashedly check him out; again. His jeans mold to his body perfectly and showcase his sexy as sin ass. Before he exits, he looks over his shoulder and catches me checking him out. My cheeks darken in embarrassment at being caught ogling him, but clearly he doesn't mind. He winks before stepping out onto the sidewalk.

Leaning back in my chair, I pick up my coffee and take a sip. My phone pings with a text. Placing my mug down, I pick up my phone and see it's from Nadine.

NADINE

Which dress?

pic 1

pic 2

Pic one is her in a formfitting, little black dress and killer heels. The second is of her wearing an emerald green halter top with black leather pants and the same killer heels.

SIMONE

TWO…definitely two…you look smokin' hot

Aww, thanks, babe. What you wearing?

Well, after seeing your getup, I need to up my game.

PFFFT, you're hot without even trying. I'd do you if you were wearing a brown paper bag

I love you, but I'm all about the D… sorry, babe

Back at ya, now go get ready so we can get this party started and find some D

I snort-laugh at her reply.

And please don't wear a paper bag

Dammit, there goes that idea now

laughing emoji

Grabbing my things, I head upstairs and get ready for the night ahead.

Since I have time, I run a bath and pour myself a glass of wine. Adding in some jasmine scented bubble bath, I wait for it to bubble up and then climb in. Leaning back, I close my eyes and immediately a vision of Saxon appears before me... but then that vision quickly morphs into him kissing that chick on the phone from earlier, whatever the skank may look like.

Sitting upright, I shake my head of that image. "He's a player, Sim, move on," I tell myself as I lie back and stare at the wall opposite. Sipping on my wine, finally relaxing.

The bath water is no longer hot so I chug my wine and climb out. I hop into the shower where I wash my hair and shave—everything. I'm going to hook up tonight because I need to get Sucky Saxon out of my head. Why are the good-looking ones always such assholes? With his dark blond hair. Gorgeous hazel eyes. Chiseled jaw. Tight and taut ass. Rock-hard chest. "Ugh, such a shame," I complain as I turn off the water and step out. Grabbing my towel, I dry off, wrap it around my body, and walk into my closet. I stare at my clothes. "Decisions. Decisions," I singsong to myself as I decide on what to wear.

Taking a page from Nadine's book, I grab a pair of burgundy high-waisted pants, a black off-the-shoulder boho blouse, and my strappy sky-high black heels...which are surprisingly comfy for the height of the heel.

With my outfit sorted, I work on my makeup and hair. I blow-dry my locks and pull them up into a high ponytail. I curl the ends to give them a bit of bounce and adds some pizazz to my high pony. I'm not one of those girls who cakes on her makeup. I apply a tinted moisturizer, mascara, and lipstick. BOOM! Done.

Stepping into my room, I look at myself in the full-length mirror and I smile. I look amazing and I cannot wait for the night ahead. Picking up my phone, I see I have a text from Nadine.

NADINE

Be at yours in fifteen

Looking at my watch, I see she should almost be here. Grabbing my clutch, I throw in my ID, cash, keys, and a lip gloss. Closing the clasp, I exit my apartment and head downstairs.

Stepping onto the street, I see Nadine in the Uber waiting for me. She opens the door and wolf whistles at me. "Babe, you are seriously making me reconsider only liking the D, you are smokin'."

Doing a spin, I giggle. With my hand on the door, I'm about to climb in when I look to my left and freeze. Walking down the street is Saxon. Still looking sexy AF. My eyes roam over him and then I see his girlfriend behind him. I quickly smile before I climb in next to Nadine.

"Why do you look like you're about to cry?" She grabs my hand and squeezes as the car pulls away from the curb.

"Men just suck," I inform her.

"Why do men suck?"

"I met this guy an—"

"You met a guy and I'm only just hearing about him now." She shimmies in her seat to face me. "Tell me ev-rey-thang."

"It doesn't have a happy ending 'cause the jerk face has a girlfriend."

"What an asshole."

"Yep...why are the sexy ones all douche-faced dickwads?"

"'Cause men can't be, or do, two things at once," she tells me, just as the car pulls up outside Nobel's Tavern. It's recently changed ownership and had a name change. Some of the guys in our class said it's great since the new person took over and Nadine and I are giving it a go tonight. Plus, it's in walking distance so we can stagger back to my place at the end of the evening.

Linking arms together, we head inside for a night that will go down in the history books. Nadine and I drink ourselves silly. We dance our asses off and in the early hours, head home alone. No D for either of us tonight.

We drunkenly stumble out of the bar and make our way back to my place. We're giggling like schoolgirls and are about as quiet as a herd of elephants. We fall over each other in the hallway and it takes longer than necessary to open my door—trying to get the key into the lock is proving difficult—since I'm currently seeing three of everything.

I've just gotten the door open when the door to 7C opens, turning my head, I see three dark-haired figures in the doorway, well it looks like three. One of them growls, "Can you two make any more noise?"

Nadine flips the bird over her shoulder and walks, well staggers, into my apartment, leaving me in the hallway with the jerk in 7C.

Squinting my eyes, I close one and stare at the doorway, realizing it's only one person and not three and they are female. "Dath's richded comding fromd 7C," I drunkenly snarl, pointing my finger in their direction. Spinning on my heel, I walk in my door, and hear someone say, "Please don't piss my neighbors off."

Slamming the door behind me, I stumble and fall to the floor. Spinning around in anger when you're three sheets to the wind wasn't a good idea because now that I'm lying down, I can't get back up.

Nadine's feet appear in my vision and she starts cackling like a hyena. "You look like a turtle on its back."

Managing to lift my hand, I flip the bird at her. "Fuckded you'd, Nadsd," I say, as I finally manage to roll to my side and lift myself onto all fours. Taking a deep breath, I push myself up and manage to stand.

There's three of Nadine and my stomach rolls. Covering my mouth, I drunkenly stagger-run to my bathroom and throw up. Resting my arms on the seat, I purge and purge. I throw up all the alcohol I consumed. Lifting my head, I groan before I lie down beside the toilet.

The last thing I remember before I pass out is thinking that the tiles are cold.

Waking the next morning to a buzzing sound from nearby, I groan in pain. Opening my eyes, I squint at the brightness. Lifting my arm, I cover my eyes and my hand hits something cold. Turning my head, I see the bottom of the toilet and that's when I realize I'm on the bathroom floor.

"I'm never drinking again," I moan.

Every muscle in my body aches. My mouth feels like the bottom of a dirty ashtray. My hair is a matted mess.

"You and me both," Nadine says from the doorway.

Turning my head to look at her, I groan again, but this time it's not because of how I feel but rather because of her. "How do you look like that?" I spin my finger at her. "And I look like an extra on *The Walking Dead?*"

She shrugs her shoulders at me. "I hate you," I spit at her as I lift myself into a sitting position. The room spins and my stomach rolls.

"Here, drink this," she says, handing me a glass with a pinkish brown liquid in it.

"What's this?" I ask, scrunching my face at the color of the liquid.

"A hangover smoothie. Google says it's meant to help and I have to say, I feel better since drinking it."

"It looks like baby shit. What's in it?"

"All the good shit that will make you feel better."

"Death will make me feel better," I tell her. Taking a sip, I nod. "Doesn't taste too bad but seriously, what's in it?"

"Kale, blueberries, banana, ginger root, coconut water, almond milk, and oats."

"And I had all that shit in my fridge?"

"You do now," she says, taking a seat on the edge of the bathtub. "Now drink up and then I'll take you out for a greasy breakfast."

"You're the best," I honestly tell her.

"I know but you need to have a shower first because you smell like a homeless person."

"You say such nice things to me." I blow her a kiss and then I drink my hangover smoothie and surprisingly, I do feel marginally better when I'm finished.

Handing her the empty glass, I stand up, strip off, and climb into the shower. The hot water feels amazing on my skin and when I step out, I feel more like a human and less like a swamp haggy.

I pull my hair up into a messy bun and dress in leggings, a slouchy 'Good Vibes Only' T-shirt and my Chucks. Grabbing my sunglasses and clutch from last night, Nadine and I head out for a greasy breakfast.

6

Soraya left Sunday evening to head back to Los Angeles, with a promise to come and visit me again soon, as long as I promised to visit L.A. and see the family. Reluctantly I agreed because it's been a blast hanging with her, but man, living with a chick is hard work. Who knew they needed that many products to get ready with?

The last few days have been quiet without her, but after all the partying that we got up to—much like my neighbour, my liver and body are enjoying the downtime.

I can't believe how much I miss my sister, her mess and all.

Taking a seat at my desk, I grab my headphones, open my MacBook and bring up my Aussie playlist on *Spotify*. Clicking on "Khe Sanh" by Cold Chisel, it begins to play and I sing along as I go through my check list. I get to it and pay the outstanding bills, wages, and finalize orders for the week. The paperwork associated with owning the bar is a drag but it's worth it to be my own boss.

I've moved on from my Aussie list and now I'm singing along to "Don't Stop Believin'" by Journey when I hear a banging. Saving the file I was working on, I walk to the door. Pressing pause on my Beats, I open it up but no one's there. A door down the hallway slams and I hear a muffled, "Fucking asshole."

Shaking my head, I go back to my desk and sit down. My stomach rumbles and I look to the clock and see that it's nearly three. Closing the lid on my computer, I grab my wallet and phone and head downstairs for a late lunch.

I'm in line waiting to order when the hairs on my neck stand on end, *she's here*. Spinning around, I smile when I see Simone entering Mugz. "Good afternoon, Elevator Girl."

"Just Saxon," she says with a head nod, using her nickname for me too.

"Hey, Saxon," the barista, Anastasia, coos. She flirts with me every time I'm in here and I ignore her advances each and every time, but she just won't get the hint. "The usual?"

"Yeah," I say, nodding my head, "and a large latte for the lovely lady behind me."

She looks over my shoulder at Simone and eyeballs her.

"Thanks, Just Sax," Simone says. "I'll grab us a table." It almost sounded like she said just sex and now my mind is in dirtyland as I watch her saunter over to an empty table. My eyes drop to her ass and I hold back a groan. She's wearing leggings and a slouchy shirt, it's a simple outfit but she looks a million bucks.

"That'll be nine fifty, Sax," Anastasia says.

"It's Saxon," I growl, my tone harsher than I intended, but this chick really needs to take a hint. Her eyes flit over to Simone and then back to me as if to say, 'How come she can call you Sax?' Handing her a ten, I drop a few coins in the tip jar and walk over to join Simone. She's grinning. "What?" I ask as I take a seat across from her.

"You just broke that poor girl's heart."

"And her dad would break my face if I went there. She's jailbait."

Simone laughs. "So, Just Saxon," she emphasizes my name, "how was your day?"

"Productive. Yours?"

"Ugh," she groans, "my jerk neighbor keeps playing loud music."

"Some people are such inconsiderate assholes."

"Yep," she agrees, then my name is called. Standing, I collect our coffees and place Simone's in front of her.

"How did the exams go?"

"Pretty good I think. My friend Nads—"

"Nads?" he questions.

"Nadine." He nods and I continue, "Nads and I are heading out this weekend to celebrate them being over but we kinda already did that last weekend."

"You should swing by my bar."

"You own a bar?"

Nodding my head, I'm about to tell her all about it when her phone rings. She pulls her phone out and her face morphs into a megawatt smile. "Daddy," she says in greeting, but that smile quickly disappears.

"Yes, this is she." She nods her head and intently listens to the person on the other end of the line. Her eyes well with tears as she blubbers, "Is...is he okay?"

Reaching over, I grab her hand for support. She squeezes in return and that small gesture means everything. I'm only getting one side of the conversation but I can tell, it's not good news.

"Okay, I'll be there as soon as I can." She hangs up and stares into space.

"Everything okay?" I ask her.

She shakes her head, "Yes. No. I don't know. My...my dad was in an accident."

"Is he okay?"

"They say he's okay but I need to get home and see him."

She pulls her hand free and grabs her bag and coffee. She leans down and kisses me on the cheek. "Thanks for the coffee." Before I can say anything, she's racing out of the coffee shop and toward the elevators.

Standing up, I race after her but by time I make it to the lobby, she's nowhere to be seen. Why do we keep getting interrupted like this?

7

SIMONE

Stepping into the elevator, I dial Nadine. "Hey, hey, sexy lady," she sings in greeting.

"It's my dad," I wail in the phone. As the words pass my lips, I begin to cry.

"What's wrong?" she asks, her voice pitched and on high alert.

"He was in an accident. I need to get home to Chico."

"I'll get my dad's car and pick you up within the hour."

"I can't ask you to do that," I reply in protest, as I enter my apartment.

"You didn't ask, I offered. Now pack, get coffees, and I'll see you in an hour."

"You're the best," I tell her honestly, wiping away a stray tear.

"I know. See you soon."

Walking into my bedroom, I grab my bag and start throwing in clothes, underwear, and toiletries. To be honest, I have no clue what I pack. Just as I'm zipping up my bag, loud music comes from next door. "Fucking asshole," I grumble, as I slide my bag over my shoulder and head down to Mugz to grab coffees for Nadine and me.

When I step into Mugz, I look around but Saxon is gone. I could really do with seeing his smiling face right now, instead I'm met with a scowling barista named Anastasia, who is giving me the eye. I don't think she's my fan since Saxon blew her off earlier.

I order two venti-sized coffees and move to the end to wait.

It's quiet so Scowly McScowlerson is making them. *I hope she doesn't lace them with poison*, I think to myself. Not taking the chance, I watch her intently and luckily for Nadine and me, no poison, or spit, is added.

Anastasia hands me the coffees and I smile in thanks. Taking a sip of mine, I moan as the caffeine hits my system. Looking to her, I smile. "You're a lifesaver, this is just what I needed." Her lips lift into a small smile and then she remembers I'm the enemy and her scowl reappears.

Nodding at her, I exit Mugz and step out onto the street, just as Nadine pulls up. She climbs out and hugs me tightly. "You okay, babe?"

"As soon as I see Dad I will be." And that's the truth. Until I see him with my own two eyes, I will worry my little heart out.

"Well, in just under three hours you'll get to see him."

"Nads, what if he's not okay?" I voice, my eyes welling with tears. "I can't lose him."

"Nope," she admonishes me, "no negative thoughts. Daddy Mitchel will be okay. I feel it in my bones."

"Is that your medical diagnosis?"

"Yep," she grabs her coffee, "now climb in and let's hit the road. We might just get out of the city before rush hour."

Opening the back door, I throw my bag in and climb into the passenger seat. Once I'm all buckled in, Nads pulls out into traffic. It's busy, but not too busy, and twenty minutes later we're crossing the Golden Gate Bridge heading north.

The sun is starting to set when Nadine pulls into the parking lot at the Enloe Medical Center. I stare at the building and just sit here. "Babe," Nadine says. She reaches across the center console and squeezes my knee. "We're here."

Looking over to her, I nod my head. "What...what if I lose him? I can't lose him, he's my everything."

"Babe, Daddy Mitchel is the strongest man I've ever met. He will not be leaving this earth 'til his baby girl is a fully fledged doctor and she's given him at least three grandchildren."

A laugh escapes. "At least it's down to three now. It used to be half a dozen."

"Three sets of twins. Boom, doneski," she says on a laugh.

"My poor hooha. Let's stick with three."

"Triplets it is then."

I chuckle, "Okay, I can do this." But I make no effort to get out of the car.

"You need to get out of my car."

"Okay, I can—"

"Do this. Yes. Yes you can, now seriously, get the fuck out of my car."

Taking a deep breath, I open the door and climb out. Nadine joins me and we walk inside, where I'm immediately hit with that hospital smell. Most people hate it but not me. I live for the scent, which is lucky since I want to be a doctor...and I have the chicken scratch handwriting to go with it.

Putting one foot in front of the other, I slowly walk over to the information desk. My heart racing the closer I get.

"Can I help you?" the nurse asks me.

"My dad, Gaven Mitchel, was brought in earlier. I'm his daughter, Simone. And this is my best friend, Nadine Prescott, or Nads as I call her. We just drove up from San Francisco, I'm at UCSF there and—

Nadine interrupts, "Babe, she doesn't need your life story."

"Ohh, yeah, right, sorry. I just want to see my dad."

"He's up on the third floor. The nurses there can direct you to his room. I'll call and let them know you're on your way up."

Nodding my head, I smile. "Thanks."

Nadine and I walk over to the elevators but they're taking too long so we enter the stairwell and walk up the three flights to where my dad is.

Pulling the door open, it bangs against the wall, the sound echoing in the stairwell and onto the floor. "Oops," I whisper, as I walk over to the nurse's desk. The lady behind the desk looks up. "You must be Gaven's daughter?"

"Simone," I tell her. "This is my friend, Nadine."

"Nice to meet you both. Follow me and I'll take you to your dad."

"Is he okay?" I ask.

"He has a broken leg and a few bruises, but he'll make a full recovery. We're just keeping him overnight due to his age. Your mom is in with him now."

"My mom?" I question her. "My mom's dead."

"Ohh," she says. "He's in there." She points to the door next to her and makes a quick getaway.

"Mom?" I whisper to Nadine.

She shrugs at me.

Knocking on the door, I push it open and step inside. Dad and a lady quickly pull apart. His eyes widen as if he was caught with his hand in the cookie jar. I scrunch my face up at that analogy because I don't want to be thinking of Dad and a woman's cookie jar.

"Baby Girl," he says, his voice a little loopy.

"He's a bit out of it from the pain meds," the lady with him says. She stands up and walks over to me. "I'm Maree, your dad's—"

"—lady friend," he singsongs to the room. "But don't tell Simone, I don't want to upset her. I'll always love my Meredith but Maree, she's something special to me." He falls silent and when we look over, he's out cold.

"Pain meds are like a truth serum for some," Nads says, trying to hold back a giggle at Dad's honesty right now.

"I'm Maree," his lady friend says, offering me her hand. "It's nice to finally meet you. I'm sorry you found out about us like this."

"It's fine." And it really is, I'm happy Dad has someone special in his life again. "I just want him to be happy."

The three of us fall silent. The only sound is the beeping of Dad's heart rate monitor and his snoring. The three of us step out into the hallway. "What happened?" I ask Maree.

"He was on his way home from the store when a drunk frat shithead ran him off the road."

My eyes widen, Mom died in a car accident and Dad could have died in one too. "And you're positive everything is okay? There's no internal bleeding? No internal injuries? His blood pressure is stable?"

"Ummm, I think so," Maree says.

"I need to see his doctor." Spinning on my heel, I walk to the nurses' station. "I need to see Dad's doctor. Now," I tell her, my voice firm.

"Can I help you with anything?" she asks.

"I need to know he's okay. I need to know he's not going to leave me alone. I...I can't lose my dad. He's my only parent," I tell her, tears streaking down my cheeks.

Arms wrap around me from behind. Spinning around, I break down in Nadine's arms. "I can't lose him, Nads," I cry into her shoulder.

Lifting my head, I wipe away my tears and race back into Dad's room. Falling into the seat next to his bed, I clasp his hand in mine and let it all out. I uncontrollably cry, holding my dad's hand.

"Please don't cry, Baby Girl," Dad says, his voice croaky.

Lifting my head, I stare at him. "I can't lose you, Daddy."

"I'm not going anywhere anytime soon. I'm hanging around until my baby girl is a fully fledged doctor, and you've given me at least four grandbabies."

A laugh escapes me. "Nads said that earlier."

"Your friend is wise."

"She sure is," I agree, nodding my head. "Are you sure you're okay?"

"Promise, Baby Girl. I'm a little sore but fine."

...two days later

"Are you sure you'll be fine without us here?" I ask Dad for the billionth time.

"Yes, I'll be fine. Maree is here to help me if I need it, and there's also the EMTs if it's really bad."

"Don't even suggest that to the universe. No more hospital visits for you."

"So I can't visit you when you're officially Dr. Mitchel?"

"That's completely different. No hospital visits as a patient. Got it?"

"You're bedside manner needs work, Baby Girl," Dad teases. "Now go on, get out of here."

"Are you sure?"

He nods. "I'm sure, besides, if you stay and keep baking like you have been, I'll end up the size of a house."

A laugh breaks free when I think about all the baking I've done in the last two days. I did go a little crazy, but it was a good distraction, and what can I say, I love to bake; it reminds me of times with Mom before she died. Leaning down, I hug him tightly. "I love you, Daddy."

"I love you too, Baby Girl."

"Bye, Daddy Mitchel," Nadine says, pushing me aside so she can hug Dad goodbye.

I turn to Maree. "It was lovely to meet you. Make sure he rests," I remind her.

"I'll do my best but he's not a very good patient."

"I heard that," he chortles.

"You were meant to," Maree sasses back.

"I don't like the two of you together, you gang up on me," he whines.

"Awww, is the poor old man getting picked on?" Nadine teases.

"Hey, I thought you were on my side...and less of the old man stuff."

She shrugs and looks to me. "Ready?"

No! "Yep," I say, letting the 'p' pop.

"Let's do this then." Nadine blows Dad a kiss and heads to the car.

"Are you sure—"

"Go!" Dad yells. "I'll be fine."

Giving him one more hug, I hold on longer than necessary and then I head out to the car.

Three hours later, Nadine drops me off and when I step into the lobby, I grin when I see a sexy someone exiting the elevator.

8

SAXON

Stepping into the lobby, I look up and smile when I see Simone. "Elevator Girl, you're back," I make my way over to her, noticing she looks tired. "How's your dad?"

"He's doing good. He actually forced me to come back here."

"Is that a good thing?"

"I don't know," she sadly replies with a shrug of her shoulders.

"I'm sure he would have asked you to stay if he needed you."

"You haven't met Gaven Mitchel, he'd give you the shirt off his back and freeze. His heart is the biggest I know, he hates putting people out and he definitely hates asking for help."

"Sounds like someone else I know."

"You know all that after two coffee dates?"

"I'm pretty good when it comes to reading people."

"Is that so? Okay then, Mr. 'I'm pretty good when it comes to reading people,' read me."

"You're exhausted but if your dad called right now, you'd turn right back around and go to him." She nods at my words. "May I suggest, a bubble bath and a glass of rosé. Then bed, where you'll sleep for twelve, maybe fourteen, hours. Tomorrow when you're refreshed you can go to Mugz. Mainline coffee and study. Even though you've finished your current exams. You're getting prepared for the next round."

"So basically, you think I look like shit right now. That I stink and need a bath and wine will help me to relax. And that family, studying, and coffee are life?"

"I didn't say you look like shit, if anything, right now, you look beautiful. Tired but beautiful nonetheless."

She bites her bottom lip and I want nothing more than to bite it too.

"Smooth, Saxon, very smooth," she says, a smile graces her gorgeous face.

"I'd love to hang but I need to get to work. How about coffee tomorrow?"

She nods. "I'd like that."

"Give me your phone," I demand, with my hand outstretched and a pleading look on my face.

Pulling it from her pocket, she unlocks it, and hands it over. I program my number and send myself a text. "You have my number and I have yours."

Handing it back, our fingers briefly touch. A jolt of electricity sparks between us and from the look on her face, she felt it too. "I'll text you tomorrow when I'm free."

She nods and smiles. "I look forward to it."

Turning around, she walks toward the elevators. "It's good to have you back!" I yell out.

She looks over her shoulder and I notice her cheeks are pink and she's glowing like an ethereal angel. "It's good to be back."

She steps into the elevator and leans against the side wall. I can clearly see her from where I'm standing, but she can't see me. She rests her head back and closes her eyes. Her lips lift into a grin and it's the most beautiful sight I've ever seen.

The elevator doors close, cutting me off from the beautiful image of Simone. With a pep in my step, I head to Nobel's for the evening shift. I'm excited that she's back and for what the future may hold for myself and Elevator Girl.

9

Running into Saxon just now was a nice surprise but the most surprising thing, how excited he was to see me AND he asked me on a date...kinda...sorta. Sure, it's only coffee at Mugz but it's a start, right?

Entering my apartment, I dump my bag in my room and grab my phone. Flopping onto my bed, I call Dad.

"Hey, Baby Girl," he answers on the second ring.

"Hey, Dad. We made it back safely."

"Glad to hear it," he replies, and I notice that his voice isn't as perky as when I left earlier. I knew I should have stayed because he sounds tired. He needs me.

"How you feeling?" I ask him, knowing that regardless of how he feels, he's going to say he's fine but he shocks me with his honest reply.

"I feel like a bus has hit me."

"SUV," I tell him and he laughs.

"Fine, I feel like an SUV hit me but I do feel better than I did two days ago. Just tired."

"I should have stayed."

"No, you need to be in San Francisco and focus on your studies."

"But—"

"No buts, Simone Meredith Mitchel."

"Ohh, you middle named me."

"Yes, I did. Now you listen to me, I'll be fine." He places emphasis on those last three words. "AS I said when you left, Maree is here and if things turn to poo poo, I will call you or the EMTs."

"Promise?"

"Promise," he tells me.

"Good. Now run a bath, drink that pink shit you like, and chillax."

A laugh escapes me. "What's so funny?"

"Saxon said the same thing when I ran into him when Nads dropped me off."

"Is that the boy you're smitten with?"

"I'm not smitten."

"The lady doth protest too much, methinks," Dad says in a terrible Shakespearean accent.

"The lady doth not," I retort. "And on that note, I'm going to do as my daddy suggests."

"Has hell frozen over? You're doing as I suggested."

"Hardy har, old man."

"Less with the old, hey? First Nadine calls me old, now you." He pauses. "I love you, Baby Girl."

"I love you too, Daddy-o. I'll call you tomorrow."

"I look forward to it. Enjoy your bath and sleep tight."

"You too, Dad...well, not the bath but sleep well."

"Bye, Baby Girl."

Hanging up from Daddy, I decide to do exactly as he, and Saxon, suggested. Walking into my bathroom, I run a bath, light a few candles, and bring up my chillaxing playlist. While the bath is filling, I head into the kitchen and pour a glass of rosé. How Saxon knew rosé was my drink of choice I will never know, but it's kinda awesome he knows me in that way.

With my glass in hand, I head back to the bathroom and strip off.

Climbing in, I moan as I sink into the steaming hot water. Closing my eyes I take a sip of wine and lie back. A vision of Saxon appears before my eyes. He's in the tub with me, staring intently at my naked body. My clit begins to throb at the thought of him here with me.

Placing my glass onto the bath table caddy thing, I slide my hand between my legs. My fingertip brushes over the sensitive bundle of nerves and I quiver. Slipping my finger between my folds, I let out a guttural moan as I press inside. Lifting my other hand, I fondle my breast. Tweaking my nipple between my thumb and forefinger, the sensation builds between my thighs with each tug.

Pressing a second finger in, I increase my speed and pinch my nipple harder. The pressure builds and builds until I explode like fireworks on the Fourth. Bright white lights appear behind my closed lids and I cry out as ride through my climax.

Collapsing back, I slide down and submerge myself under the water in the tub. Breathing out deeply, bubbles rustle the liquid around me. I can't believe I just jilled off to a vision of Saxon. Coffee tomorrow with him is going to be awkward now.

Breaking the surface, I sit up, reach out, grab my glass of rosé, and take a big sip. Followed by another. Lying back, I leisurely sip my wine and think about what I want to do about the Saxon situation.

10

LAST NIGHT WENT FROM A HIGH, RUNNING INTO Elevator Girl, into a shitshow of epic proportions. Seems everyone's drinks were laced with asshole juice....or it was a full moon. The patrons were on fire last night with the insults, sass, and general assholeness.

By time I arrived home, later than usual, I'm even more pissed off. Grabbing my *Beats*, I log into Spotify and hit play on "Hey Ya" by Obadiah Parker. I love the Outkast version but this guy's version is edgier and different.

With music blaring in my ears, I start to tidy up, getting on top of the laundry I let go while Soraya was here. Thinking of my sister, I smile and then I remember that I agreed to visit her and the rents soon. Not looking forward to that at all, I'd much rather have a root canal than spend an evening with Mom and Dad.

With everything washed, folded AND put away—go me—I walk back into the living area and notice a sheet of paper on the floor near the door. Bending down, I pick it up and read.

Show Some Courtesy,
Jerk!

—Your Pissed-Off Neighbor

Opening the door, I look into the hallway but it's empty. Surely I didn't miss this when I walked in. Someone must have dropped it off just now, but then again, I was in a mood when I got home and I may have missed it. But why would someone drop a note like this off so early in the morning?

Turning the music off, I sigh and place my Beats on the coffee table. Pulling my shirt over my head, I flop onto the sofa in just my jeans. Flicking on the television, I find something to watch. I'm too wired to sleep. I keep staring at the clock, waiting for it to be an acceptable hour to text Simone for our coffee catch-up.

Standing up, I walk over to the window and pull back the curtain. I stare out at the cityscape. The sun shines between the buildings, basking the city in a golden glow, and it gives me hope that today is going to be a better day than yesterday.

Looking at the clock on the wall, I see that it's almost seven. That's an acceptable time to text, right? I can't wait any longer so I pull out my phone and send her a text.

SAXON

Good morning, Dr. Elevator Girl. Tell me when you're free for coffee???

Placing my phone down, it beeps immediately.

ELEVATOR GIRL

Morning, Just Saxon. Coffee sounds great. 30 mins?

My face morphs into a grin when I see she wants to meet soon.

It's a date...see you soon **coffee cup emoji**

With a pep in my step, I jump into the shower to freshen up, and then I head down to Mugz to meet up with Elevator Girl.

11

SIMONE

GAH, THE JERK IS AT IT AGAIN. I'M AWAKENED TO the sound of "Hey Ya" but it's not Outkast singing. I have no idea who it is but it's not bad...then I remember it's 4-freakin-a.m. and it's not time to be appreciating loud music.

Banging on the wall, I wait for the tunes to be turned down, but as usual, nothing happens. Lying here, I stare at the ceiling. My anger building with each passing moment. How can someone be so blatantly rude?

My anger reaches fever pitch. Since my banging isn't doing anything, it's time to take action. And since I'm a chicken and not one for confrontation, I grab a sheet of paper, my black marker, and I scribble a note to the arrogant jerk in 7C.

Wrapping my robe around me, I walk into the hallway and slip it under his door. Banging my fist on the wood when I stand upright again. Clearly he doesn't hear me because he's currently in the middle of a rock concert. I love music but not at four in the morning.

Stomping back to my apartment, I slam my door in anger and throw myself onto my bed. Pulling my pillow over my head, I try to block out the tunes coming from 7C, but it's no use, I'm too worked up to sleep so I climb out and get dressed.

Making myself a coffee, I grab my Kindle, curl up on the window seat with my mug of liquid gold, and I lose myself in *Beautifully Mine* by my new favorite Aussie author, Tara Lee. This Bishop guy is totally swoony. He reminds me of another swoony guy I know, just without the mafia elements...well, I think Saxon has no ties to the mafia but in this day and age, anything is possible.

I'm so lost in the words that I jump when my phone pings with a text. Looking up, I see the sun has risen and I'm almost finished my book. I was so lost in the world of Bishop and Callie that time just flew by.

Grabbing my phone, I grin when I see it's a text from Saxon. I also see that the smart-ass man saved his name in my phone as 'Just Saxon.'

After agreeing to meet him downstairs in thirty, I brush my teeth. Once they are sparkly clean, I grab my bag and head down to Mugz.

Pushing open the door, I step inside and inhale deeply. Opening my eyes, I smile when I see Saxon is sitting at a table by the window. Two coffees in front of him. On autopilot, I head toward him.

"Good morning, Just Saxon" I say in greeting, as I take a seat across from him.

"Good morning, Elevator Girl."

"Is that for me?" I ask, pointing to one of the coffees in front of him.

He shakes his head. "Nope, they're both mine," he teases, before sliding a mug across to me.

"Rough night?" I ask him.

Wrapping my hands around the ceramic, the warmth from the mug seeps into me. Bringing the cup to my lips, I inhale before I take a sip.

"How do you make drinking a coffee look so erotic?"

"Didn't realize I did that."

"You make lots of things look sexy."

"Like what?"

"Breathing. Walking. Laughing but most of all, drinking coffee."

"Real smooth, Just Saxon, real smooth."

"Just stating the truth," he says nonchalantly. "How's your dad?"

"I spoke to him last night before I did as you suggested, he's doing okay. Maree is there to help him."

"You call your mom Maree?"

I shake my head. "She's his girlfriend, I guess. My mom died when I was little."

"I'm sorry to hear that."

"Thanks," I sadly say, there's not a day that goes by that I don't miss her. "What about your parents?"

His face scrunches up. "We aren't close."

"How come?"

"Long and complicated story."

"Well, I don't have anywhere to be, and I've been told I'm a good listener. How about we move over to the comfy sofas and you can tell me all about them?"

"I'd like that," he says.

12

SAXON

I'd like that, what the hell? I willingly want to talk about my family, *what's going on?* I think to myself as we walk over to the sofas. I can't believe I've agreed to tell her all about my family. But what's more shocking is that I WANT to talk to her about them. I want to talk to her about everything. I want to know all there is to know about Simone Mitchel aka Elevator Girl.

Folding myself onto the couch, I tuck one leg underneath me and lean back. She mimics my pose, our knees not quite touching, but I can feel her presence regardless. "So tell me all about your family, Just Saxon."

"Before I start, can I say that I love you calling me Just Saxon."

"Well, I kinda love you calling me Elevator Girl." She reaches over and places her hand on my knee and the contact sets every nerve ending in my body alight. I've never had a reaction to a woman like this before, and if I'm honest, I love it as much as when she calls me Just Saxon.

"Well, now that we have the names out of the way, tell me all about yourself."

Taking a deep breath, I let it out. "I'm the black sheep of the family."

"How so?"

"I'm not a lawyer like the rest of them."

"What do you do?" she asks me.

"I recently bought a bar."

"Wow, that is very different from being a lawyer but I'm guessing you were different, per se, prior to that?"

"Very much so. My older sister and brother followed the set path. Me? I took off for a gap year after finishing school. That year turned into seven. I've only recently returned to the States."

"Where did you run off too on your gap seven?" I laugh at her 'gap seven' remark.

"Australia, Europe, and then back to Australia."

"Wow, that's like on the other side of the world."

"You've never been?"

She shakes her head. "Nope."

"Have you traveled overseas?"

"Does Cabo count?"

"Kinda sorta." I tell her. "Maybe one day I can take you to Australia."

"Nope, no way in hell. Everything that moves there can kill you and I don't feel like dying anytime soon."

"I survived."

"Yeah, but you're six foot of muscle and hotness."

"You think hotness would save me from a drop bear?"

"Drop bears aren't a real thing."

"You sure about that?" I tease.

"I may be blonde, but I'm not a dumb one. Drop bears are a myth. Just like the abominable snowman, Nessie, and unicorns."

"Unicorns are too real."

"Show me one and I'll believe you."

"If you believe, you will receive."

I make a mental note to buy a unicorn for her.

"Mythical creatures aside," she says, "why the animosity with your parents?"

"I was never good enough for them. There's quite an age gap between my brother, sister, and me. I was an accident and therefore I was already mud in their eyes."

"That's not possibly true."

"It is. Sanford and Judy Nobel had a plan and I wasn't in their plan." Silently I add, *I'm still not in their plan.*

"Sax," she says, her voice sad and soft, "I'm sorry that you grew up like that." She rests her hand on my knee again to show her support and that small gesture means everything.

"Luckily for me, I have Marshall and Grayson. And my sister."

"And me," she adds, squeezing my knee to reiterate her support.

"And you."

We stare at one another.

A force overtakes my body and I lean toward her. Seems the same force has latched on to her too because she also is leaning in. Cupping her cheek in my palm, I gently press my lips to hers. She grips my cheeks and deepens the kiss.

Our tongues slip and slide together.

Our hands grip each other tightly.

As first kisses go, this one is pretty amazing.

Breaking the connection, I rest my forehead against hers. "Wow," my hoarse voice rasps.

"Wow, indeed," she agrees. Pulling away, she leans back into the sofa. Her cheeks flushed. Her lips plump. She's staring into space.

"What's on your mind, Elevator Girl?"

"That was some kiss," she says, looking to me. Her eyes all dreamy like and probably very similar to mine right now.

Nodding my head in agreement, I stare intently at her. Our eyes glued to one another. We're both silent, but it's not awkward like some silences can be. I'm about to ask her to dinner over the weekend when my phone rings. Pulling my phone from my pocket, I see it's Dad. I've been avoiding his calls for the last few days.

"Do you need to get that?"

"It's my dad," I tell her.

"Are you going to answer?" Shrugging, I look back up at her. "Answer and get it over with. Rip that Band-Aid off as they say."

"A medical metaphor?" It's her turn to shrug. "Fine." I answer the call, "Dad."

"So you are alive," he says as he way of greeting.

"Hello to you too, Dad. I'm well, thanks for asking."

"Don't be smart with me, boy. Your mother and I are hosting an event next month on the twentieth and we require your presence."

"Want or need?" I snap at him. My anger building the longer this conversation continues.

"Does it matter?" That's his go-to response and yes, Dad, it does fucking matter. Just once. *I'd like to be invited because they want me there, not because they need me*, I think to myself, but I've never had the guts to stand up to them.

"So you need me there. Figures," I say, my voice cracking on the word figures.

"Saxon—"

"I'll be there," I interrupt. "Bye, Dad." I hang up before I say something that I'll regret. I stare at the coffee table, hurt. Defeated. Just once, once, in my life, I'd like to be wanted because I'm Saxon, not because I'm Saxon-fucking-Nobel.

A body slides next to me and a hand rests on top of mine, squeezing. "You okay?" the soft voice that instantly calms me says.

Turning my head, I stare into her blue-gray eyes. I see concern reflecting back at me. I shrug. "I feel like I always do after being summoned to Mount Doom."

"Mount Doom, really?"

"It feels like Doomsville when I'm there."

"When's the last time you saw your parents?"

"The day I left for Australia."

"You haven't seen your parents in seven years?"

"Yep," I reply, letting the 'p' pop, and then a bright idea forms. Before I have time to process that thought, I blurt it out, "Hey, what are you doing next month on the twentieth?"

Her eyes widen at my request, hell, I'm surprised too. Why would I want to subject her to an evening with Judy and Sanford Nobel? Before she can think about it, I quickly add, "Forget I said anything, I wouldn't subject my worst enemy to an event at my parents' place."

While at the same time she says, "Tell me the date again and I'll see what I can do?"

"Really?" I ask her, my voice an octave higher from the shock of her agreeing.

She shrugs. "Friends help friends, right?"

"We're friends, are we?" She nods. "Just friends?"

Again she shrugs but from the sultry look she's giving me just now, I'm pretty sure we're more than 'just friends.'

13

Saxon asking me to accompany him to his parents' place was a shock. I mean, we've had coffee a few times and now he's inviting me to meet his family. Who does that? My immediate thought was how do I turn him down without hurting him? But when I remember the pain on his face from the call with his father, I changed my mind and said I'd check. From what he just told me about his family, I don't want him to hurt anymore.

I think I shocked him when I offered to check, hell, I know I shocked myself but friends are there for one another and that's what we are, friends...or maybe we're more. I don't know. Before I can address our relationship status, the alarm on my phone goes off.

"That's my alarm to get to school," I inform him, as I silence my phone.

"Same time tomorrow?"

"I'd like that," I honestly tell him.

Standing up, I grab my bag and look down at him. "I'll see you tomorrow, Just Saxon."

"See you tomorrow, Elevator Girl."

With a goofy grin on my face, I exit Mugz and head toward campus.

I'm in la-la land when someone taps me on the shoulder. I scream in fright and when I turn around, I see Nadine. "Dude, you were off in the clouds."

"Sorry, I've had a weird morning."

"Tell me about it," she says. Looping her arm with mine, we continue down Parnassus Ave, and I bring her up to speed on my jerk of a neighbor and my coffee date with Saxon.

"So you're telling me, you agreed to meet the rents and you've only had coffee a few times?"

"Yep," I reply, nodding my head and still in shock that I agreed.

"Wow, this guy must be gorgeous then."

"You have no idea, Nads. He does things to my body, and clearly my brain, that have never happened before."

"I'm so happy you're going to get some D."

"We've kissed, there is no D in the V happening anytime soon."

"His D is totally going into your V by the end of the week."

"I'm not a ho, I don't just jump into bed with people...I'm not you," I smartly say.

"Hey, I'm not a ho. I just appreciate the D."

"By definition a ho."

She looks at me and relents. "Fine, I'm a ho."

"And I wouldn't have you any other way."

For the next week, Saxon and I meet for coffee each morning before I head to school and he heads home to bed. He's fast becoming a highlight of my day.

My jackass neighbor is still a jerk and we have rotated back to the beginning of his playlist. I'm tempted to speak to the super about his loud music, but I've been so focused on school and waiting to see if I've been accepted into the residency program that it really isn't at the top of my priority list right now.

This morning, not only did I have to listen to Journey telling me to "Don't Stop Believing" I also had to listen to giggles from the jerk's latest skanky ho. It's been quiet on the giggle front but this morning, he's clearly making up for lost time—jerkface.

Saxon texted me while I was getting ready stating that he couldn't make it for coffee this morning. I was bummed that he cancelled. But at least I still have tonight to look forward to. Nadine and I were both, yes both, accepted into the emergency residency program starting next June. Since today is Friday, Nads and I are heading out to celebrate.

Daddy-O was over the moon when I called him yesterday with the good news. He reckons that Mom was looking down on me and made it happen, but whatever and however it happened, I'm over the moon and one step closer to officially becoming a doctor.

I'm waiting for the elevator when the door to 7C opens. "I'll be back in a bit," a feminine voice says. When I look up, I see the stunning blonde from the other week step out.

"Morning," she cheerfully says, stopping beside me.

"Morning," I reply. She vaguely looks familiar but I can't place where else I've seen her.

The elevator arrives and we both step in. It's silent, I'm tempted to ask her to tell her boyfriend to stop being an asshole, but I haven't had any coffee yet and it's not her fault she's hooking up with a loser.

"Have a great day," she croons, as she races through the lobby and heads outside.

Deciding to mix things up, I head to the Starbucks on the way to campus. With a venti mocha—see, mixing things up—I head toward the library. I love this building and I'm in the mood to people watch this morning.

Pulling up a chair, I watch everyone go about their morning. Making up elaborate stories about what's going on in their lives.

My classes pass by quickly and before I know it, I'm headed back to my place. I stop at the liquor store and grab a bottle of wine to drink while I get ready for my night out with Nadine.

Realizing that I haven't eaten since this morning, I enter Mugz and smile when I see Saxon sitting alone. Walking to the counter, I order my coffee and sandwich and head over to him.

Tapping him on the shoulder, he looks up and when he sees me, his face brightens. Seems he's just as happy to see me too. I was worried after he blew me off this morning, but clearly, I had nothing to worry about.

I've just sat across from him when the blonde from this morning races up to him and shouts his name. My eyes widen when it hits me, Saxon is the jerk in 7C.

14

SAXON

"Saxon," Soraya shouts as she races over, "You're needed at Nobel's," she breathlessly pants.

"Why didn't they call me?" I ask her.

"Your phone is going straight to voicemail. They called me so it must be urgent. They really need you now."

Looking to Simone, I tell her, "I'm sorry. I have to go."

"It's fine," she says, but I know that when a woman says fine, it's anything but. Her gaze keeps flicking between Soraya and me, and I can't read her expression.

"Now, Sax," Soraya growls. Grabbing me by the arm, she pulls me up and drags me to follow her.

Looking down at Simone, I smile; upset that our coffee date has been cut short. "Thanks for having coffee with me, again." Turning on my heel, I follow Soraya out of the coffee shop and we head to Nobel's, but I keep playing the look on Simone's face when I left over and over.

Ten minutes later, I follow Soraya through the front doors of my bar and stop mid-step when I see Grayson and Marshall leaning against the bar.

"Surprise," they say in unison when they see me.

"What are you guys doing here?" I ask, walking over to them. We do the manly, one-arm, backslap hello hug thing.

"The new season starts in a few weeks, so we thought we'd come here, see the new bar, and have one last hurrah before the racing craziness begins.

"Dude," I say to Marshall, "you going to win that trophy again this year?"

"You know it, Sax," he says with a cocky grin, but in reality, it's not cocky at all. Marshall Kerr is one of the best drivers ever.

"Damn right you will, I bet my left nut you'll be on that podium at the end of the season."

"I don't want your nut, or the bet. I'm not jinxing anything." He superstitiously knocks on the wooden bar twice.

Grayson and I laugh. Marshall is extremely superstitious when it comes to racing and his career, but I guess it's helped him since he's where he is already in his profession.

"How about we take this back to my place?" I ask them both. "Or do you two assholes want stay and hook up?"

"Your place," they say in unison.

"It freaks me out when you two assholes do that. Let me just check in with Tara and then we can go."

"You tapping that?" Marshall asks, head nodding toward Tara, my bar manager.

Shaking my head, I reply, "Nope, I don't shit where I eat."

"I would, in a heartbeat," Grayson exclaims before chugging back the last of his beer. Soraya gives him a look but he doesn't seem to notice.

"I'd have a go, too," Marshall says, but we all know he's full of shit. Marshall is happily married to Eloise and no one will come between the two of them. Not even her asshole abusive ex could.

"Dude, I'm sure your wife would have something to say about that." At the mention of his wife, a goofy grin appears on his face.

"I'm free and single to mingle," Grayson interjects, and I swear I hear my sister growl at that statement.

"My staff is off-limits," I snarl.

"You're no fun," Grayson pouts, crossing his arms, garnering a glare from my sister.

"Dude, there's plenty of other chicks in San Fran. Just charm them with your killer smile and you'll be set."

"You're just jealous that I have women throwing themselves at me."

"Yeah, that's it," I tell him. I notice as he says this, his eyes are locked on someone behind me. Looking over my shoulder, Soraya standing behind me and then I see Tara over near the bar. Snapping my head back to him, I warn again. "Not my staff." He flips me the bird and I head over to Tara.

After finalizing things with Tara, we leave Nobel's and make our way back to my place. We decide to walk since my bar is only a few blocks away.

"Hurry up, asshole," Marshall shouts as we turn the corner onto my street.

Flipping him the bird, I shout back, "My sister and Grayson are behind me, why aren't you yelling at them?"

Reaching him, he slings his arm around my shoulders. "Because, genius, I can't get into your building, therefore, I need you and not them."

The two slow-asses join us and there's tension between them. We enter the building and luck is on our side, the elevator is waiting so we climb in and head up.

Entering the apartment, I head to the kitchen to get drinks for everyone. Beers for us boys and wine for Soraya. With everyone's drinks in hand, I head into the living room and hand them out.

Taking a seat on the sofa, I look to Soraya. "Were you in on this?"

"Yeah. I was," she proudly announces, clinking her glass with Marshall's, but the look she gives Grayson is anything but happy.

"What's up with you two?" I ask, flicking my finger between Grayson and my sister."

"Nothing," they both say quicker than ever, which totally indicates that something is going on.

I eye them suspiciously. "Put away the Sherlock Holmes look, little brother. Nothing is going on between me and him." The venom she attaches to the word *him* causes me concern.

"Yeah, dude, listen to your sister, besides, she's not my type," he retorts, but from the tone of his voice, something is going on there. And if the look my sister sends his way when he says that is any indication, there is definitely something going on there.

"Seems she's now into the dick pic type," I tell everyone.

"Saxon," she shouts at me. "They don't need to hear that."

"Agreed," Marshall confirms.

Grayson stays suspiciously quiet, but from the murderous look on his face at the mention of Soraya's dick pic, something is definitely up.

"I'm going to bed," she tells us, and before anyone can say anything, she's walking down the hallway to the room she's been staying in. The door slams with a force that shakes the apartment.

Looking to Grayson, I stare him down. "What's going on, and don't tell me nothing?"

"Seriously, dude, nothing is going on between me and your sister." I swear I hear him whisper quietly, "Not anymore."

Not wanting to ruin the limited time we have together over something that may or may not be true, I let it go. The three of us continue to drink and talk shit 'til the wee hours of the morning.

Climbing into bed after a few too many brewskis, I realize how much I missed those assholes. It's time for me to surprise them now, and I think I know how to surprise Marshall, but how do I surprise Grayson?

15

SIMONE

She's the woman from 7C.

She's the giggler.

Which means he's the jerk from 7C.

Saxon is my loud, music playing jerk of a neighbor.

My eyes flick between the two of them but before I can say anything and confront the jerk, he races off with his skank. I should have known it was all a farce and too good to be true. I wonder if the story about his family is even true? He seemed shocked to be caught with me just now—that's because clearly I'm the other woman—hence why he raced away with her.

"Stupid. Stupid. Stupid," I mumble to myself.

Leaning back, I keep playing the scene from now over and over in my head. *Of course he's a player as well as an inconsiderate jerkface,* I think to myself as I finish my coffee. My mood has soured drastically since he left with his skank.

Standing up, I head upstairs and when I enter my apartment, I text Nadine.

SIMONE

Men suck

NADINE

Yeah they do **wink wink**

This isn't in a good way. Coffee boy is the jerk in 7C

My phone immediately rings. "Coffee boy is asshole boy? Please explain!" she shouts down the phone.

"I ran into coffee boy. Then his skank came. He looked shocked and then he left with her."

"How does that tie in to 7C asshole boy?"

"The blonde skank, just now, is the one I've seen leave his place on multiple occasions now."

"Holy shit," she huffs out.

"I said a few more choice words than that but holy shit covers it."

"Okay, new plan for tonight. Ice cream. Tequila and a *Scream* marathon."

"Sounds perfect," I quietly say, then I add, "How was I so stupid?"

The first tear drops. "You are not stupid, Simone Mitchel. He's a dickwad, cockfuck, dickhead asshole who doesn't deserve you."

"But I really liked getting to know him."

"He obviously wasn't the one."

"Why are the hot ones always such..." But I don't get to finish that sentence because I break down and cry.

"On my way," Nadine says and she hangs up. She's my bestie for a reason and I'd be lost without her.

Throwing my phone onto the coffee table, I curl into a ball on the sofa and I continue to cry. I cry for being played. I cry for what could have been, and I cry for being a fool and falling for a sexy lying jerk with kinda good taste in music.

A knock at my door startles me. Wiping my face, I wander to the door and when I open it, it's Nadine. Before she steps inside, she flips the bird to the door of 7C and then envelops me in a hug. Bottles in the bags she carries clink and smack me in the back, but I don't care. I wrap my arms around her and cry some more.

You'd think I'd be all out of tears but they continue to flow like an avalanche down my cheeks.

Nadine pulls back. "Okay, tequila and then more tequila."

"I like the sound of that," I blubber, wiping my nose on my sleeve.

"Ugh, that's disgusting," Nadine says, as she steps around me and heads toward my kitchen. She returns with a bottle of tequila, lime, salt, and two shot glasses.

"I love you," I tell her, as I take a seat cross-legged on the sofa. Nadine places everything on the coffee table and sits on the floor, resting her back on the sofa and stretching her legs out under the table.

She goes about filling the shot glasses. Reaching forward, I grab a glass and slam it back. "More," I say as the tequila burns my throat.

Without saying a word, she fills my glass again. "To assholes," she declares, raising her glass and drinking.

"To assholes," I sadly say and drink my shot.

There's a knock at the door. I squint at it, willing it to open but I'm not a witch so it doesn't. Standing up, I stumble to the door and swing it open. I'm met with a guy staring at me. "Mind turning the music down?"

"Nope," I tell him. "Justd giding the assdhold a tasted."

"What?" he snarls.

I shrug and stumble. A just as drunk Nadine joins me. "Sup," she says to our guest.

"Just turn it down," he requests again, his tone meaning business.

Saluting him, I slam the door in his face and Nadine mouths 'asshole,' as I walk back over to her. Before I get to her, "Black Betty" by Ram Jam comes on. Both our eyes widen. She jumps up, grabs my hands, and we start dancing/jumping about my living room. Drunkenly we try to sing along to the music but I think we giggle more than sing. The song changes to "Baby Got Back" by Sir Mix-a-Lot and like the drunk twits that we are, we giggle, dance, and sing to our hearts' content.

After our impromptu dance concert finishes and we collapse onto the sofa, I pass out from the alcohol and emotional wipeout.

When I wake the next morning, I'm still on the sofa, Nadine is nowhere in sight. Sitting up, I groan. My neck is sore, my stomach is churning, and my heart still hurts that Just Saxon and the jerk in 7C are one and the same.

16

Last night with the guys and Soraya was just what I needed. I haven't had a night to chill like that since I took over Nobel's. It felt weird to be home and in bed at an early hour, but it's made me realize that I need to find a better work-life balance.

My neighbor made quite the racket in the wee hours of the morning. Grayson went next door and told them off but they sounded quite inebriated. I'm pretty sure his words fell on deaf drunken ears, because when he returned the music got louder, as did the giggles and then it was silent. Dead silent.

That's when the guys and I called it a night. I crawled into bed and blissfully dreamed of Elevator Girl.

Loud voices from the living room wake me up the next morning. Sitting up, I blink away the sleep, only to hear the front door slam. Climbing out of bed, I pull on my jeans from last night and a fresh shirt. Walking into the living room, I see the back of Grayson as he races out of my apartment.

Marshall walks down the hallway. "What's with the commotion?" he asks, pulling a Schofield Racing T-shirt over his head.

"Beats me, but I need coffee."

"Me too, you got any?" he asks.

"I do but there's a coffee shop downstairs, wanna head there instead?" And maybe I can see Elevator Girl too.

"Sounds good to me," he agrees.

We both put on our shoes. Grabbing my wallet and keys, we head out.

The elevator takes forever to arrive. We step in and make our way downstairs. When I step into the lobby, I smile when I see Elevator Girl. She looks stunning this morning with her golden locks down and a sexy as sin sundress hugging her curves in all the right places. And then over her shoulder, I see the last thing I expect to see.

17

Finally I manage to stand up and I shuffle slowly, very, very slowly, into my room. I find Nadine in my bed, sound asleep. As usual, the bitch looks like a freakin' model, and me, my usual swamp hag look.

Walking into my bathroom, I turn the faucet on to brush my teeth. Lowering the lid on the toilet, I sit down and begin to brush. I think to myself at least this time, I was on the sofa and not on the toilet floor; maybe next time I'll make it to my bed.

Standing up, I spit and rinse. Walking back into my room, I see Nadine awake so I climb onto the bed next to her.

"Ugh," Nadine groans, "I think I'm dying."

"We can die together," I reply. "I'm never drinking again."

"Famous last words."

Shuffling down, I flop to my back and stare at the ceiling. Then I turn my head and look at Nadine. "Last night was meant to be a celebration, but instead it was a commiseration over a lying, cheating, sexy jerk."

"Well, since it's Saturday, why don't we celebrate today and tonight?"

The thought of more alcohol has a lump forming in the back of my throat but from the look on her face, I don't think alcohol is in her plans. "What do you have in mind?"

"Spa day followed by drinks—"

"Ugh, no drinks."

"You need drinks to celebrate but we don't have to go hard-core like we did last night. Maybe just a bottle... each."

"My poor liver," I say on a laugh as I sit up.

"Trust me, after our spa day, you'll be ready to party like it's nineteen-ninety-nine."

"We'll see," I tell her as I climb off the bed. "I'm gonna grab a shower while you book the spa and run downstairs to get coffee."

"Why do I have to get the coffee?"

"Because you look fucking stunning and I look like a swamp rat. How do you do that every time we drink?"

"I'm just clever."

"Well, you suck."

"How about we both shower, go down together, and then we can start celebration day?"

"Fine," I grumble, but I do like the plan of sticking together.

Walking into the bathroom, I close the door behind me and turn on the faucet. While the water heats up, I strip off and when the room is all steamy, I climb in.

Ten minutes later, I'm drying myself and I feel refreshed. It's amazing the difference a hot shower makes when you feel like death. I can only image how I'm going to feel after being pampered later.

Nadine borrows a dress of mine and we look like matchy match twins. Both in sundresses and flip-flops but we don't care.

Grabbing our things, we head out and call the elevator, lucky for us, the doors open immediately and we step in. The doors close and as the car makes its descent my stomach rolls and I feel like I'm going to throw up, damn tequila.

Stepping out, I look up and see Saxon's lady friend—skank—fighting with a guy when he grips her cheeks and slams his lips to hers. The kiss is hot, it's a kiss that should be shared in private. It reminds me of my kiss with Saxon and a pang of hurt hits my heart.

The elevator doors open again and then from behind me, I hear a growl followed by the words, "What the fuck is going on?"

Spinning around I see it's Saxon. My eyes widen and I think, *Ohh shit.* "That's our cue to leave," I whisper shout to Nadine.

Yanking on her arm, I drag her out of the lobby and onto the street before the situation we just witnessed descends into chaos.

"Why did we have to leave? That was gonna get good," she whines, as we walk down Parnassus Ave.

"The chick kissing that dude is the one that Saxon left with yesterday afternoon. She's his skank and it seems she's stepping out on him. Just like he was on her."

She stops in the middle of the sidewalk, causing people to dart around us. Her eyes widen at my revelation. "We totally should have stayed, that was definitely gonna get interesting, like *Days of Our Lives* interesting."

Interesting is a mild way to put it and even though he was being a dog by having coffee with me and kissing me, I do feel for the guy. Catching your girlfriend kissing someone else has gotta be rough.

"Nope, no way," Nadine says, "you don't get to feel sorry for that jerk."

"How did you know I was thinking that?"

"Babe, I know you better than you do, and I can see it written all over that pretty little face of yours."

"I sometimes hate that you know me so well."

"No you don't, you love me, but seriously, Sim, this doesn't change anything. He's a cheater and the jerk in 7C."

Nodding my head, I don't say anything. I just keep walking and thinking about the clusterfuck this has all turned into.

18

SAXON

Storming across the lobby, I march toward Soraya and Grayson and bellow, "What the fuck is going on?"

The two of them pull apart and sheepishly look at me. Both of them stare at me wide-eyed and open-mouthed, like they've been caught with their hands in the cookie jar. Ugh, bad analogy, I don't want to think of my sister's cookie jar.

Grayson snarls, "Fuck off, Sax, this is between me and Raya."

While my sister timidly says, "Saxon, it's not what you think."

"What I think, dear sister, is that my ex-best friend was kissing my big sister."

"Saxon," she pleads, "it's nothing."

"Nothing, really?" Grayson snaps at my sister, ignoring me. He grabs her shoulder and spins her to face him. "Raya, please?" he begs her. "Please don't do this."

"I...I...I can't," she cries, before pulling away from him and racing out of the building.

He goes to chase after her but I reach out and grab his arm, squeezing tighter than necessary. I'm kinda pissed right now. "You need to start talking and you need to start talking right fucking now because I'm five seconds away from aquatinting your face with my fist. Repeatedly."

"Tequila, we need tequila but since it's too early, coffee will have to suffice until it's an acceptable time for tequila," Marshall says, trying to break the tension that's building between Gray and me right now. "I'm gonna go order us some."

"Thanks, man," Grayson says to a retreating Marshall. I don't blame the guy for leaving because this situation is tense. Grayson turns his gaze to me. "Dude, I'm head over heels, ass over tits, in love with your sister."

Blinking rapidly at him, I try and process his words. *I'm head over heels, ass over tits, in love with your sister.*

"Come again?" I ask. "Did you just say that you're head over heels, ass over tits, in love with my sister?" I'm still blinking rapidly at him, hoping that with each blink his words will make sense in my brain.

He nods. "I love your sister, man. I thought she loved me too, but clearly we're on difference pages since she's hooking up with dick pic boy."

"It all makes sense now. My mention of the dick pic is when she and you turned sour last night." I pause. "How long has this been going on?"

"I've always thought she was hot, have you seen her?"

I raise my eyebrows at him. "Dude, that's my sister you're referring to."

"Anyway," he says, ignoring my sister comment. "We met in Vegas a few months back. She was there for a friend's wedding and I was there with work. We had a few drinks, and I don't know, something changed between us. She was no longer Saxon's big sister, she was just Soraya. Sexy, hot Soraya. One thing led to another and—" A growl breaks free. I don't want to hear about my best friend and sister getting it on. "Okay, yeah, well you can guess what happened. Then work got busy with the new season around the corner and she thought I was blowing her off, when in fact, it was just bad timing. We kept missing each other. Things went quiet until she called a few weeks ago with the plan for this. I thought it would be great, I get to see you and hopefully sort things out with her, but seems she's moved on."

"Dude, I should kick your ass for this."

"I know. It goes against bro code and all that, but your sister, she's pretty fucking amazing."

"And pretty pissed off right now," I tell him.

"And that."

We both fall silent. "What are you going to do?"

"I want her to be happy so I guess I have no choice but to let her be happy with dick pic guy."

"Fuck that," I snarl, "my sister deserves better than dick pic guy, and to be honest, there's no one better suited to her than you."

From the look on Grayson's face, I think I shocked him, and if I'm honest, I totally shocked the shit out of myself with my reply. "That's all well and good, but I don't think she's on board with it."

"That kiss was hot," Marshall says joining us with a tray of takeout coffees. "She's still on board with it."

"Really?" Grayson asks, sounding hopeful.

"Yep, now, let's get breakfast then we can worry about playing matchmaker."

"Totally not what I thought we'd be doing today, but I hate seeing my sister upset. So looks like 'Operation Get-Grayson-and-Soraya-Together' is a go."

Walking into Mugz, we grab a table. Marshall hands out the coffees and the guys look over the menu. We each hop up and order some food.

After devouring breakfast, we order more coffee and then head back upstairs to brainstorm.

We've just nutted out the plan when the door to my apartment opens and in walks a red-eyed Soraya, she's been crying. I look to Grayson and scowl at him, but his eyes are focused on my sister.

He jumps up and races over to her. "Raya, babe," he says, gripping her cheeks in his palms. "I'm sorry I was a dick. Nothing was really official between us so you have every right to receive dick pics from another guy. I'd prefer you receive one from me—" A growl slips through my lips, I really don't want to hear about this. Grayson and Soraya in unison flip me the bird. "You are everything, Soraya Nobel, and if you'll officially have me, I'm yours."

"What about Saxon?" she tearfully asks him. Grayson wipes away a tear from the apple of her cheek.

"He's my friend and your brother, but you mean more to me than he does." He looks over his shoulder at me. "Sorry, dude, it's the truth." He looks back to Soraya. "So what do you say? Wanna give this a go? Officially?"

"I do, but what if it ruins your relationship with Sax? I can't be the reason you two have a falling out."

"Not gonna happen, 'cause you and I are it, babe. I think I've loved you since you wore that bright pink bikini to your parents' Fourth of July party."

"I was fifteen."

"That's how long I've been crushing on you. I never thought I'd get a chance so I've never told anyone."

"Grayson Walker, you are full of surprises," she tells him, before pressing her lips to his. The two of them kiss and make up. They continue to smooch as if no one else is in the room. I look over to Marshall.

"So, how's the weather today?" I joke, trying to change the topic of conversation and not think about my sister and best friend making out a few feet away from me.

Grayson and Soraya pull apart and laugh. He slings his arm around her shoulder and pulls her into his side. He presses a kiss to her temple and I see nothing but adoration for my sister in his gaze. He laces their fingers together and drops into the armchair, pulling Soraya onto his lap. Guess I better get used to seeing them all over each other.

With the air now clear, the four of us decide to head to Nobel's for a few quiet drinks.

Stepping outside, I look up and stop mid-step when I see a sexy as fuck Simone doing a spin in front of a car. From where I'm standing, she looks fucking amazing. *She's totally going to hook up with someone tonight.*

Before she climbs into the vehicle, she looks up and our eyes meet. She smiles at me, and fuck me sideways, it does things to me that a smile never has done before. She scowls and then climbs in, leaving me confused.

Marshall slings his arm around my shoulder and we start walking down the street, talking shit. This weekend has been full of surprises, and the coming week has just as many in store for me.

19

I'M SO FREAKING RELAXED RIGHT NOW, THIS MUST BE what floating on a cloud is like. Every inch of my body was touched in some way, even my nether regions. Nadine convinced me to get a Brazilian and I can say, never again. Holy burning flaps, Batman, even now just thinking about it has my lips tingling...and not in the good sexy way.

We head back to my place and change clothes. Nadine borrows my LBD and I slip into a purple halter dress that hugs my curves and makes the girls look much bigger than the measly 'B' cups.

Once dressed, we link arms and head downstairs, jump into our waiting Uber. I see Saxon as I climb into the car and my heart aches at what could have been. I offer him a smile and climb in. We head to Nobel's for a few—and I mean a few—quiet drinks.

Walking in, I grab a booth while Nadine heads to the bar, she's on drinks duty.

Grabbing my phone, I flick through Insta when I hear a voice. That voice causes the hairs on my body to stand on end and my pulse to quicken. Slinking down, I try and hide myself. Why is he here?

Nadine places a pitcher of beer and two glasses on the table. "Why you hiding?" she asks, as she starts to pour our drinks.

"He's here," I whisper-shout.

"Who's here?" she questions, looking around the bar, and I know when she finds whom I'm hiding from.

"He's with her," she says, her words shocking me.

"Whaaat?" I screech, sitting up in the booth, I look over and yep, he's sitting at the bar with his cheating girlfriend. "You catch your girlfriend kissing someone and you go to a bar with her, what the hell is up with that?"

"Beats me," she says with a shrug. "But I will say, he is fine...mighty, mighty fine."

"And a liar. And a cheat. And a right royal doucheface."

"Why are the hot ones always like that?"

In unison we singsong, "'Cause they're douchfaces."

His laughter fills the air and a pang of hurt slices through my chest. How can I be so heartbroken when I hardly knew the guy? "Do you want to get out of here?"

Did I mention that my bestie is the best bestie around? She knows me too well. I look across at her and surprising myself, and her, I shake my head side to side. "Nope, I'm not letting that douchehole ruin our night."

Lifting my beer, I raise it up in a toast. "To doucheholes and their skanks."

"To doucheholes and their skanks," she repeats, we clink glasses and then drink. A shadow appears at the end of the booth and without turning my head, I know it's *him*. His scent invades my senses and causes my insides to quiver. Clearly, my libido hasn't gotten the douche memo.

"Hey," he says, and that one word turns me into a gooey pile of mush.

Closing my eyes, I take a deep breath. Lifting my gaze, I look up. "Hi," I timidly whisper, hating that my body is still reacting to him like it always does, even though we know he's a jerk. As I stare at him, my emotions are all over the place. I'm about to say something when his skank skips over, "Sax, dude, you need to see this." She pulls on his arm and pulls him away. I don't know if I'm grateful or pissed off.

My eyes wander over to Saxon and his skank and my heart hurts. I really thought I'd found a nice guy, but it seems I was wrong.

"How about we take this back to your place?" Nadine says, breaking my woe is me moment. Looking at her, this time, I nod in agreement.

Standing up, she links arms with me and we exit Nobel's. Before I step outside, I look back over my shoulder. My gaze connects with his. His eyes roam over me and even though I'm ten feet away, my body heats at the intensity in his stare. *He really is a player*, I think to myself. Here he is, eye fucking me and his skank is right beside him. Shaking my head, I turn and follow Nadine back to my place.

Along the way, we stop at the market on the corner and grab supplies—wine, ice cream, and chocolate.

When we get back, we both change into our pajamas and set up camp on the sofa. We start watching the *Hostel* movies, nothing like a slasher film to get your mind off the seriously hot coffee shop guy, who also happens to be the jerk in 7C.

It's the wee hours of the morning by time Nadine and I crawl into my bed. No sooner do I turn off the lights and the music from next door starts up.

"Ohh, wow, he really is an asshole," Nadine says.

"Yep," I reply, letting the 'p' pop.

Nadine and I lie here for a few hours, the music still pumping. "I've had it with this," I growl. Climbing out of bed, I put my slippers on and angrily march over to 7C. Banging on the door, I continue to hit the wood until it swings open.

I'm met with *her* but before she has the chance to say anything, I shout, "Turn the fucking music down, you inconsiderate jerkholes!"

Shocking me, she says, "What music?"

20

SAXON

I'M IN MY ROOM WHEN I HEAR A BANGING AT THE front door. Looking at the clock, I see that it's not quite six. Who would be here this early?

Walking out, I smile when I see it's Elevator Girl but when she says, "Turn the fucking music down, you inconsiderate jerkholes!" My eyes widen when I realize ***I'm*** her asshole neighbor.

Soraya asks what music and my girl growls. Yeah, she's my girl. Even if she ditched me tonight. I was hoping to have a few drinks with her, but she left as soon as I saw her. And I will say, she looked fucking hot in that dress. It melded to her body perfectly; I was hoping that I'd get the chance to peel it off her delectable body, but fate had other plans.

"Are you fucking serious right now?" She protests, "You can't hear Adele crooning about rolling in the deep?"

I press pause on my music and lower my Beats around my neck and walk over to them.

"Hey," I say, hoping to diffuse the situation.

"Turn the fucking music down," she snarls again.

"I have my Beats on, surely you don't have supersonic hearing?"

"The whole fucking floor can hear it."

With them around my neck, I press play and realize that it's blaring through the stereo and not through my headphones. "Shit." Looking to Soraya, I ask, "Why didn't you tell me the music was blaring?"

I'm so embarrassed right now. Ever since I moved in, I've been pissing off my new neighbors, especially the sexy girl in 7B, who also happens to be the beauty from the coffee shop and my Elevator Girl.

"Dude, I learned to tune out your music years ago," she says with a shrug.

"Ohh," I say, then I look to my sexy pissed-off neighbor. "Look, I'm really sorry. As you can see," I point to the headphones around my neck, "I've been wearing Beats, which seem to have not been connected."

"Likely excuse. Just stop being a jerk. Some of us need our sleep, as well as peace and quiet to study." Before I can say anything to defend myself or apologize, she turns on her heel and storms back to her apartment. Slamming the door behind her.

"Fuck me," I groan.

"Dude, you have noooo freakin chance now," Soraya says from behind, slapping me on the back to reiterate how screwed I am when it comes to Elevator Girl.

"I would have if you'd told me my music was blaring at all hours."

"Dude, how did you not realize your speakers weren't connected?" She doesn't let me reply before she adds, "Besides that, you really shouldn't listen to music through headphones that loud anyway. You'll go deaf."

Flipping her the bird, I stomp into my bedroom, slam my door, and throw myself onto my mattress. Rolling to my back, I stare up at the ceiling. I need to come up with a way to make this up to her, and the rest of the floor. I can't have the girl in 7B, aka Elevator Girl, angry at me.

21

It's been three days since kissgate and two days since the showdown over his music, and I can say, it's been two glorious days of radio silence from 7C. I haven't seen him in the coffee shop and there's been no loud music blaring at stupid a.m. Seems his Beats excuse was true but what I don't get is, why she's still there?

He caught her with another guy, maybe they have an open relationship and that's why he was pursuing me? Whatever the case, I'm not into the kinky poly threesome shit. Sure, I like watching threesome porn but watching and partaking, are two very different things.

I've been avoiding Mugz like the plague because I can't handle seeing Saxon right now. The last few times I've seen him, my heart hurts at all the things that could have been between us. I know it's silly to be this upset, but I really thought we had a connection, but clearly, I thought wrong.

I'm so lost in my head and what-ifs about Saxon and me that I'm not watching my surroundings. I'm about to step into the street when I'm suddenly yanked back. Arms slide around my waist and I'm pulled out of harm's way. My heart is racing and when I spin around and look up, I see Saxon staring intently at me.

"Are you okay, Elevator Girl?"

"My name's Simone," I snap at him, "and yes, I'm fine. You can let me go now." He removes his hands and I immediately feel the loss.

"Okay," he says. "You must have been in your own little world. I've been calling your name for the last block and then you nearly stepped in front of that red truck. Are you sure you're okay?"

"I'm..." But I'm at a loss for words, I don't want to voice my hurt to him. Shaking my head, I sigh. "I'm fine. Just a lot going on."

"My sister always says that when a woman says she's fine, she's anything but."

"Your sister is wise," I tell him. We fall silent and like usual, it's not awkward. It's oddly perfect but I know that everything is not perfect. "I have to go," I say, breaking the silence. Stepping around him, I pause and turn back to face him. "Listen, Saxon, I deserve better than to be a side piece so this," I flick my finger between the two of us, "it won't ever happen."

"What?" he questions, he seems shocked at my declaration.

"This. Us. It's, we, I'm sorry but whatever you're thinking, it will never happen."

Turning back around, I look both ways and after a car passes, I cross the street. Reaching the other side, I turn around, "Saxon!" I shout. He lifts his head and stares across the street at me. "Thanks for saving me."

He nods and smiles. We stare at each other, our gaze locked firmly on one another. Even though we're on a busy street, everything around me fades away. It's just the two of us staring at one another. If this was a cheesy RomCom, we'd both walk to one another and we'd kiss passionately in the middle of the street. A bus passes between us and when it's gone, so is he.

With a sigh, I turn around and head back to my apartment.

Waiting for the elevator, I look over at the entrance to Mugz and a wave of sadness washes over me. That sadness disappears when the elevator doors open and out *she* steps. "Hey," she says all nicely.

"Hi," I reply, because Dad always taught me to be polite but my tone is anything but. Thankfully my phone rings, saving me from an unwanted conversation. Pulling my phone from my bag, I see it's Dad. "Hey, Daddy-o."

"What's wrong, Baby Girl?" he asks.

"How did you know something's wrong?"

"I know that tone. Who broke your heart?"

"Daddy," I say on a blubber.

"Ohh, Baby Girl," he consoles, his tone that endearing fatherly one.

"He wasn't who I thought he was."

"Then he wasn't the one. When you know, you know."

"But the coffee shop version could have been. The cheating, loud music playing neighbor, not so much."

"Huh?" he asks, clearly confused.

Stepping out of the elevator, my eyes drift to the door of 7C as I walk to my own. With a sigh, I unlock mine and tell Dad all about the guy in 7C. Both versions.

"Well, it sounds like he doesn't deserve you," he tells me. "No boy who hurts my baby deserves her."

"I didn't think the coffee shop version would."

"Mr. Hyde's girlfriend probably thought the same until she met Dr. Jekyll. Speaking of doctor, how long 'til you start the program?"

"Next semester," I tell him, excitement building at what lies ahead.

"Your mom would be so proud of you."

"You think?"

"I know so."

"And how do you know so?"

"Because I am. You are the best version of you and as a father, that's all I've ever wanted."

"Dad," I croak on a sob. "I love you."

"Back at ya, Baby Girl."

We say our goodbyes. After hanging up, I walk over to the mantel and pick up the last family photo of the three of us. "I love you, Momma Bear," I say to the picture. Kissing my fingertips, I place them over her. At times like this, I wish she was here to give me advice. Dad is great and all, but I need motherly advice right now.

A knock at my door startles me, looking to the door, I know it's him without even getting up, but I'm not in the mood to face him so I ignore the knocking. He finally realizes I'm not home because it stops, and then I hear a door opening and closing in the hallway.

Later that evening, a knock comes again. Looking through the peephole, I see him standing there. He's wearing a long-sleeved black Henley pushed up to the elbows. His hands are tucked into the pockets of his jeans. He looks hot.

The elevator doors open and out walks *her*. "Hey, dude," she says to him.

"Hey," he replies, and that one word has never sounded so sexy. "You ready?" he asks her.

"I just need to change."

"Okay, well hurry, we'll be late otherwise."

She walks toward their apartment and he knocks on my door again. "Asshole," I mumble, as I continue to stare at him through the peephole.

A few minutes later, *she* remerges. He smiles at her and then throws his arm around her shoulders. The two of them walk toward the elevator, laughing and looking like the picture perfect couple. Seeing that cuts me. I should be over the hurt by now, but whenever I see them together, it feels like my heart splits open again. Will I ever get over him?

22

It's been a few days since I saved Simone from getting taken out by the truck and it's been radio silent ever since, but after what she said, I'm not surprised. I've played those words over and over in my head.

This. Us. It's, we, I'm sorry but whatever you're thinking, it will never happen.

Why all of a sudden is she not interested? Is she scared? Did I come on too strong? What caused this about-face, I really thought we had a connection.

I've sent her texts, lots of texts and I know they've been read.

SAXON

Please talk to me. I miss you.

What can I do to fix this?

Please, don't shut me out

Elevator Girl, please....

But there's one text that I write and delete over and over.

~~*I love you*~~

So I settle on a safe one.

I miss you.

Then for a few days I go with generic boring ones.

Good morning, beautiful. Have a great day!

Nite, babe

I miss you

Coffee isn't the same without you

I've dropped by a few times but nothing. I know she's there; I can feel her presence. I've never felt a connection like this with a woman before, but I feel it all with her. Her shutting me out is killing me. I don't know what I've done to piss her off. Well, obviously there's the music mishap but it's more than just that. But what?

Waiting for Tara, I order two to-go coffees before we head into the bar to do a stock check. Looking up, I see Simone's friend walk in. I stare at the door behind her, hoping to see my girl, but it appears she's on her own today.

"Hey," I say to the friend as she lines up next to me. She looks at me and if looks could kill, I'd be dead. "Have I done something to piss you off?"

"Really?" she snarls at me. "You really have to ask?" I nod because I literally have no clue what I've done to warrant this anger. "You really are a piece of work. Just stay away from my friend."

She spins on her heel and storms out. Leaving me standing here confused as hell. Placing my order with Anastasia, I step to the side to wait and then I feel her. Turning around, a smile graces my face when I see her walk in. She looks around and when her eyes land on me, they widen and she stops mid-step.

On autopilot, I walk over to her. "Afternoon, Elevator Girl."

She stares at me, her gaze shooting daggers at me much like her friend's only a few moments ago. The moment is interrupted when flirty Anastasia, walks over. She slides her hand along my arm before handing me my coffees. Simone's gaze homes in on her hand on me and her anger increases.

Thankfully, Tara arrives. "Ready to rumble?" she says sliding in next to me. Simone's gaze flicks between Anastasia and Tara, her face scrunches in disgust. She quickly turns on her heel and storms out of Mugz, forcefully pulling the door open, causing it to smash into the wall.

"What was that all about?" Tara asks, taking one of the coffees from me.

"Beats me," I honestly tell her, completely confused over the events just now.

Tara and I head out and Anastasia purrs, "Bye, Sax."

"It's Saxon," Tara snarls on my behalf and I can't help but laugh. The only person I like calling me Sax is Simone, but she seems to still be pissed over the music debacle.

As Tara and I head to Nobel's, I ask her. "Hey, if you inadvertently pissed someone off, how would you say you were sorry?"

"By saying 'I'm sorry' to them."

"Over and above that."

"What did you do?" she asks. "Is it to do with the babe who hightailed it out of the coffee shop?"

"Yeah, she's my neighbor.." As we walk, I fill her in on the coffee dates and the Beats incident.

"You know you shouldn't listen to super loud music like that with headphones on?"

"Oh my God, you sound just like my sister."

"She's smart. Like me."

"Whatever. Can you help me apologize?"

"Flowers is always a good apology."

"That's a little cliché, isn't it?"

"You wanted my help, I say flowers."

We arrive at the bar and start on the inventory. I'm in the back when Tara comes in with my laptop. She hands it to me and I see it's open to the florist on the corner's webpage. "Flowers," she whispers.

Taking Tara's advice, I order a bunch of bright and colorful flowers, hoping to brighten her day. On the card, I go with, "I'm Sorry. Just Saxon."

When I arrive home, I see the bouquet I sent sitting at my door in a heap. It looks like she threw them at my door. Clearly she's still pissed and clearly Tara was wrong, flowers didn't fix this.

Scrunching my face, I pick them up and walk inside. What have I done to piss her off?

23

SIMONE

For the last five days, I have received a bouquet of flowers at the same time each day. And like I do each time, I throw them at his door and then slam mine.

I've received multiple texts ranging from good morning to I miss you, and others begging for me to let him in. It's getting harder and harder to ignore him. I really like the coffee shop version of Saxon, but it's hard when he's also the guy in 7C. How are they the same person?

A knock at my door for a second time this afternoon startles me. Shuffling over, I swing it open and find Saxon standing there with today's destroyed bunch in his hands.

"Ohh good, you got my gift," I say through clenched teeth. My traitorous body reacts to his nearness. Even though it's been a week since I've seen him, my body buzzes at being this close to him.

"These are actually for you."

"Well, I don't want them," I reply, crossing my arms, but all that seems to do is push my boobs up, and of course, his eyes drop to them. *Pig.* "Haven't you gotten the hint yet that I'm not interested?"

"You're interested."

Shaking my head, I glare at him. "Nope, definitely not interested."

"You love me," he cockily says, crossing his arms to mimic my stance, and of course, my eyes drop to focus on his muscular arms.

"No, I loathe you," I spit at him. Then I add, "And your shitty music and your cocky playboy persona."

"Playboy? Really?"

"Really, really," I matter-of-factly state.

"I think you're jealous," he retorts, and those four words piss me off further.

"Pffft, you wish, jellyfish. How you," I circle my finger at him and point to his door, "and the nice considerate guy from the coffee shop are the same person is beyond me."

He looks confused for a beat and then says, "We're one and the same, babe."

"Don't call me babe," I snap at him.

"Babe. Babe. Babe." He taunts and with each word, my anger increases. My face is red with rage and I glare at him. The jerk has the audacity to check me out, he really is a dog.

"So mature," I growl, with an added eye roll for emphasis. I open my mouth to spew more hatred, but he steps into my personal space, slides his hand around my waist, and pulls me into him. I gasp in shock and he makes his move. He slams his lips to mine. His tongue presses into my open mouth. I refuse to kiss him back, but he squeezes my hip and a force beyond my control takes over, and I find myself sliding my arms around his neck, deepening the kiss and our connection.

Our tongues battle it out. Each fighting for domination. And the longer we kiss, my anger dissipates.

Breaking the kiss, he rests his forehead against mine. Both of us panting. "I'm a simple man, Simone. And I'm a man who isn't going anywhere. You need to accept it because you will be mine."

"Hell will freeze over before that ever happens."

"Well, lucky for me, I like the cold and you should also know, I will win. I always win, Simone, and my prize will be you."

Before I can reply, he turns around and walks toward his apartment.

Staring at his closed door for a few beats, I finally step back inside and close mine. I turn around and lean against the wood, my lips still tingling from the amazing kiss just a few moments ago.

Sliding down, I drop to my butt. It's getting harder and harder to refute his advances but each time I think maybe I can, I think of the woman leaving his apartment. "Gah, this is so hard," I hiss, leaning my head back and banging it on the door. Hoping that it will knock sense into me. FYI, it doesn't because I can't stop thinking about the guy in 7C.

After a restless night's sleep, I get up and potter around my apartment. I've been hiding out and having coffee at home, but I'm missing the hit that comes from coffee from a coffee shop. Deciding to put on my big girl panties, I head down to Mugz for lunch and a proper caffeine hit. *He* usually isn't there at this time of day so I should be safe. Stepping into the coffee shop, I inhale and instantly I feel better. The caffeine goodness infuses my soul, and I smile a genuine smile. "I missed you," I whisper to myself, when a voice from behind startles me.

"My brother's got it bad for you."

Turning around, I stare at his skank and then I register what she said. "I'm sorry, did you say brother?"

She nods. "Yeah, Saxon is my baby brother. I'm Soraya, nice to meet you again." She offers me her hand and I remember doing this with her when I thought she was one of 7C's skanks.

"I'm—"

"Elevator Girl, also known as Simone. My brother has told me quite a lot about you."

"Shit," I mumble to myself, seems that I have misread everything about this situation. Since I still don't quite believe it, I ask for confirmation. "So Saxon is your brother? Not your boyfriend?"

A snort erupts from her. "Nope, he's definitely not my boyfriend."

"So you weren't cheating on him when you kissed that guy in the lobby?" She shakes her head. "Or in a poly open relationship with him?"

"Hell no," she says, her eyes widening at the thought.

"But Saxon was so angry?"

"Well, yeah, because the guy I was caught kissing is one of his best friends." Now it's my turn for my eyes to widen as I process everything I've just heard. Walking over to a vacant table, I drop into the seat. "I've messed all this up."

"Messed what up?" Soraya says, taking a seat across from me.

"I thought you were his girlfriend. I was pissed he was flirting with me and even more pissed that he didn't dump your skanky ass for cheating with that guy when he discovered you guys in the lobby. Then I found out he was my jerkhole neighbor, but that was just a mistake over broken headphones. I thought he was flirting with me to get back at you for cheating, so I've been a bitch.

He's been trying to woo me with flowers but I've shut him down at every turn."

"You turned him down?"

"Repeatedly," I say with a shrug.

"That's gold. I don't think I've ever seen Sax work to get a girl. Usually, they just drop their panties and he has his pick of the skanks."

We stare at one another, she jumps up and stares down at me. "Okay, let me order us coffees and we can come up with a game plan for winning over my brother."

24

YESTERDAY, SORAYA DROVE DOWN TO PICK ME UP FOR the function at Mom and Dad's this weekend. She arrived midafternoon and when she knocked on my door, she had her megawatt smile and coffee from Mugz.

She didn't trust that I would attend and she'd been correct. I wasn't planning on going, not now that Simone wasn't coming. She agreed to be my plus one and save me, but that ain't happening anymore so I chickened out. Plus, I need to be here to try and get Simone on Team Saxon again. But no, my meddling sister had to drive six and a half hours and lay on the guilts. Hence, why we are now making the return trip.

Exiting my apartment, I stare at her door while we wait for the elevator. I have no clue as to why she hates me so much, what changed her mind about me? It's like the girl in the coffee shop and the girl who lives next door are two completely different people.

Meeting my sister in the lobby, she hands me a much-needed coffee, which I wish was laced with Jack. If I didn't love my sister so much, I'd totally flake on this weekend, but I did promise her I would go and I always hold true to my word. Plus she'd have my balls if I made her drive all this way for nothing.

We climb into her white Audi R8 and we head back to LA and the pits of hell, also known as the home I grew up in.

"So how's Grayson?" I ask Soraya as she pulls on to the 101.

"He's good," she says all dreamy like. "He's busy with the season. Marshall's started the season with a bang, he might actually take the title again this year."

"And you know all this after just a few races?"

"I don't know shit about racing but Grayson seems to think so."

As we continue to chat, I realize I'm a bad friend, I haven't seen any of his races this season. I really should be all over that. When I get back from hell, I'm going to be sure to catch his next race. "He sure does. The two of them are a dynamic team, add in Lincoln, his sweet-ass car and you might just be right."

"Of course I'm right, when am I not?"

"So modest there, dear sister." Looking over to her, I smile. "Thanks for this, I needed to get away for a few days and even though I'm heading toward the dragons' lair, I appreciate you."

"Mom and Dad really aren't that bad."

"Says one of the golden children. I will never live up to their expectations. You know, they haven't said one thing to me about the bar? No congrats or good luck. Nothing. The only time I heard from them was when I was summoned to this shindig."

"They care, Sax. They just don't know how to express it."

"Let's agree to disagree, as long as there's Jack, I'll be fine."

"You know there will be...I did help put this together, after all."

"What is this thing for anyway?"

"It's a fundraiser for underprivileged kids."

"Like Mom and Dad give two shits about underprivileged kids."

"It's all about appearance, you know that."

"Yep...I'm surprised they want me here."

Soraya shrugs but I think she's hiding something. Actually, now I think about it, she's been sheepish ever since she arrived yesterday. "Is something on your mind?"

"Just tonight," she says too quickly, and therefore igniting my intrigue further.

"I call bullshit, Sis."

"If you must know, Grayson and I are attending together and I'm shitting bricks over what Mom and Dad will say."

"I get that...I was going to bring Simone but that all turned to shit."

"What happened there?"

"No clue." I look out at the scenery passing by. "I miss her."

"You'll get your chance, I'm sure of it."

"What makes you so sure?"

"I just have a feeling, call it sister's intuition."

"What do you know that I don't?" I question her, she seems too chipper about all of this.

"Dear brother, I know much much more than you." I stick my tongue out at her. "Just have faith. The path to true love isn't easy, bro."

"Ain't that the truth."

"So you love her?"

"Yeah, I think I do," I say, nodding my head. "We haven't really had a chance to explore anything but from the little I know, I love that and I want to know more."

"Then give it time and it will work out. Look at Grayson and me. We finally pulled our heads out of our asses and we're happier than ever."

"I still can't believe my big sister and my buddy have been sneaking around. What else are you keeping from me Soraya Nobel?"

She mimes zipping her lips. So she IS hiding something, but what?

25

Sitting in my hotel room, my leg bounces up and down with nerves. After discovering that I had everything wrong about Saxon, his sister and I devised a plan for me to make it up to him.

Turns out his 'skanks' were his sister and bar manager, Tara. Oops, my bad. I had everything negative I thought about Saxon wrong. I just hope I haven't ruined what could be something amazing. His sister doesn't seem to think so, hence why I booked a last minute flight to LA to surprise him tonight.

This is the event that his parents demanded he attend. The event I agreed to accompany him to, and had I not ruined it all, I would have been here by his side. And hopefully, I will be.

Soraya said it's a formal affair so this morning before I flew out, Nadine met me at Nordstrom and we hit up the formal wear section. As soon as I saw the dress on the mannequin, I knew it was the one. It's bright fuchsia in color, making my blue eyes sparkle. The dress hugs my curves, finishing in fluted fishtails. The V neckline accentuates the girls and the dipped back sits just above my ass in a sexy, yet classy, way.

When I stepped out of the dressing room, the attendant's and Nadine's mouths both dropped open. I don't think I've ever seen Nadine speechless like that before, therefore I knew it was the one.

"If he doesn't take you back after this, he's a fool," she said, as she dropped me at the airport.

Standing in my hotel room, I look at my reflection. I don't recognize the girl—no—woman staring back at me. Grabbing my clutch, I order an Uber. I'm just about to head out when the room phone rings.

Walking over I answer, "Hello."

"Ms. Mitchel, your car is here," the man on the other end of the phone says.

"Excuse me?"

"Your car is here. Ms. Nobel is waiting."

"Soraya is here?"

I can hear shuffling. "Simone, it's me. Get your ass down here now and let's get this show on the road."

"Okay, I'm on my way."

Shaking my head, I hang up and cancel my Uber. Exiting my room, I walk to the elevators. Climbing in, my nerves kick in as I make my way to the ground floor. Stepping into the lobby, I walk toward the exit and when I step outside, I see Soraya standing beside a black Bentley.

"Holy shit," I scoff, "just how rich are you guys?"

"Rich enough to afford a driver."

Finally, I look to Soraya and my eyes widen once again. She's wearing a blood red halter-necked dress that's fitted across the breasts and torso before it flares at her hip and flows to the floor. "Holy shit, you look amazing."

"As do you, now, let's get you to the party so you and my brother can pull your heads out of your asses and give me some nieces and nephews."

"Wooow, hold up there, I don't even know if he wants me here."

"He does, trust me."

She opens the back door and ushers me in. Climbing into the car, I shimmy across the seat and she climbs in next to me. The door closes and the driver takes off. With each mile that we drive, my nerves increase. I anxiously bite my bottom lip, only to stop so I don't mess up my lipstick. My palms are sweating profusely. My nervousness increases when the car pulls into the Nobels' driveway. The closer we get to the house, that fluttering feeling in my stomach builds.

When my eyes land on the house before me, I turn to Soraya open-mouthed. "Holy shit," I say, all other words allude me right now.

"Wait 'til you see inside," she says, as an usher opens her door.

She steps out and I sit here, breathing deeply. The desire to tell the chauffer to drive is strong but before I can voice that, Soraya ducks down. "You ready for this?"

"No," I honestly tell her and she laughs. She has the audacity to laugh at me right now. "This isn't funny, you know."

"Yes, it is, because I guarantee you that my brother feels just like you feel right now."

"Like I want to run?"

"Yep, now come with me so you can find him and then you guys can run away together for a sexy schmexy reunion."

I like the sound of that, so I take a deep calming breath and scoot across the seat. "Okay, I'm ready."

Famous last words.

26

Soraya is nowhere to be found and if she doesn't arrive in the next five minutes, I'm out of here. Dad and Mom have ignored me since I arrived. They are peacocking all around, flaunting their wealth and being the uppity assholes that they are. Nothing has changed. Not that I thought it would have.

With a Jack in hand, I walk around the room. Smiling at the guests so as to not be rude, can't tarnish the Nobel name after all.

Standing next to the entrance—for an easy getaway if need be—I watch Mom and Dad play gracious hosts. They make me sick with their fake smiles, I can't wait to get out of here.

"Saxon," my older brother, Sebastian, says coming up beside me. "I thought Mom and Dad were joking when they said you were going to grace us with your presence."

"Anything for the family," the sarcasm heavy in my reply. No hugs or pleasantries are shared between us, we aren't close like that. Actually, Sebastian and I are nothing more than acquaintances with the same last name.

"No date this evening?" he taunts, making a show to pull Lillian Maguire into his side, making sure to flash the huge and gaudy rock on her finger in my face. Lillian and I dated in high school for like a week, like I care that he's now engaged to her. From the nonexistent smile or light in her eyes, she seems just as excited as me to be here.

"Wouldn't want to scare her off by bringing her here," I reply with an eye roll. Silence develops between us. Sebastian and I have never been close and the fact he's decided to flaunt his fiancée in my face, just shows how much we do not have in common. I'm sure Lillian will make a great wife, if you're looking for a Stepford, nineteen fifties wife.

The standoff between us is broken when from behind me, I hear a voice that I haven't heard in days. "Hello, Mr. and Mrs. Nobel."

I must be hallucinating because it can't be her, but then I hear, Soraya confirm my thoughts. "Mom, Dad, I want you to meet Dr. Mitchel, Saxon's date."

Spinning around, my eyes widen when I see Simone standing next to my sister. Rapidly I blink because I'm sure I'm seeing things. It isn't until Mother says, "Doctor," her tone high pitched and shocked. Then she turns to me and glares, "why didn't you tell us about her, Saxon?"

"I wasn't sure I could make it," Simone says, breaking the silence. "But with the help of Soraya and a last-minute flight, here I am." She looks to me. "Surprise."

On autopilot, I walk over to her. "You're here," I say, stopping in front of her.

"I'm here."

She swallows deeply and bites her bottom lip. Her eyes locked on mine. Lifting my hand, I pull it free with the pad of my thumb and rub it gently across her flesh. Cupping her chin in my hand. She leans into it, her gaze never leaving mine. "You're really here," I say again, still not one-hundred-percent sure that I'm not dreaming. Yes, her chin is in my palm right now but dreams can be vivid.

"I'm really here," she replies, lifting her hand. She cups my cheek in her palm. "I'm so sorry, Saxon," she whispers.

"Sorry for what?"

"Everything. Can you ever forgive me?"

"Forgive you for what?"

"For being a bitch."

From behind us Mom scoffs, and I can imagine in her head she'd be saying, "Society women don't speak like that." Quickly, I lace my fingers with Simone's and I hand my glass of Jack to a beaming Soraya. I pull Simone through the room and out onto the back terrace. Walking down the stairs, we round the pool and stop by the cabanas. Guests aren't allowed out here, unless it's an outdoor summer party so I know we won't be interrupted.

Turning to face Simone, I stare are at her. "You look beautiful," I honestly tell her.

"You look pretty good in a tux too."

"I fucking hate wearing a tux."

She steps to me. "Well, I fucking love it." She lifts to her toes, grips the lapels of my suit jacket, and presses her lips to mine. Her tongue licks along the seam and pushes into my mouth. Opening slightly, her tongue dips inside my mouth. My arms wrap around her waist, pulling her closer to me.

We stand under the moonlight and kiss. I don't know how long we kiss but she pulls away panting and I immediately feel her loss. We stare at one another. "Before this goes any further, I think we need to talk."

"We need to talk never ends well," I tell her, nervous as to what she's going to say.

"In this instance, I think it will."

"Okay then, talk?"

She tries to wriggle away from me. "Uhh uh," I tell her. "You'll be in my arms while we talk. I need to touch you as I listen."

"Please, Saxon," she says, and from the tone of her voice, I drop my arms and she steps back. That sinking feeling develops again in the pit of my stomach. She lifts her gaze to mine. "Sax, I made a mistake and I hope you can forgive me."

"A mistake?" I repeat. My mind is racing with what mistake she could have made. She starts pacing back and forth and it's unnerving. "What mistake?" I ask again.

"I presumed the worst of you."

"Huh?"

"I saw your sister leave your apartment early one morning. Then I saw your bar manager leave too. I thought you were a player. I now know that these chicks are your sister and bar manager. I thought you were a player, flirting with me while banging these other chicks too. Then there was the incident with your sister and Grayson. I didn't understand how you could still be with a cheater. And add in the music and I thought the absolute worst."

"But you were having coffee with me?"

"But I didn't know coffee boy and neighbor jerk were the same."

"Okay, so you pushed me away because I was apparently a player who played loud music?"

"Pretty much."

"And you thought my sister was a skank?"

"Pretty much."

"Wow," I say, dropping to the pool chair behind me. Running my fingers through my hair, I shake my head and look up at her. "How did you discover that she was my sister?"

"Yesterday afternoon, I was getting coffee and she came up behind me and said that her brother had it bad for me." Nodding again, we stare at one another. "So, do you?" she asks.

"Do I what?"

"Have it bad for me?"

Nodding my head, I stare at her standing by the edge of the pool.

"Even after I assumed the worst about you?"

Again I nod.

"Even after I threw your gifts at your door?"

Another nod.

"Where do we go from here?" she asks, walking over to me when a silence falls between us.

She stands between my thighs and stares down at me. She runs her fingers through my hair. Sliding my arms around her waist, I lean my head against her stomach. Looking up at her, I whisper, "Want to get out of here?"

27

Before he's even finished asking to get out of here, I'm eagerly nodding. Abruptly he stands up and throws me over his shoulder. He slaps me on the ass, turns, and walks—no—stalks back toward the house. He steps inside and strides through the middle of his parents' party with me over his shoulder.

Soraya claps and whistles. "Way to go, Sax," she coos.

"Soraya," Mom berates my sister for yelling uncouthly, while Dad scolds me, "Saxon, put that woman down."

"Sorry, Mom. Dad. We have to go," he says. He keeps walking and partygoers step aside to let us through.

Lifting my head, I look to his parents. "It was lovely to meet you both."

Saxon slaps my ass again and I moan, then cover my mouth in embarrassment. He walks out the front door and toward the Bentley that Soraya and I arrived in.

"Back to the hotel, please," he tells the driver, who holds open the back door for us. He places me back on my feet and grips my cheeks in his palms. He covers my mouth with his and kisses me deeply. This kiss is frenzied. Hurried. But also soft and perfect. "Get in the car, Elevator Girl."

"Or what?" I sass back at him.

"Or I'm going to fuck you on my parents' front steps." My eyes widen at his comment. My panties are soaked at the thought of him doing that to me. "Now, Elevator Girl."

Saluting him, I turn and slide into the car. He slaps me on the ass and I squeal, but my clit pulsates with want and need. Shuffling over, I watch as Saxon folds himself into the seat beside me. He turns to face me and we stare at one another, the temperature rising with each exhale. He lifts his hand and beckons me over with his finger. I return the gesture.

Neither one of us moves. We're frozen, taking each other in.

We continue to gaze at one another. "I need you now," he growls, the deep timbre of his voice vibrates through my body. Before I can process what's happening, he slides across the seat and lifts me onto his lap, sidesaddle. I'd much rather straddle him but this dress doesn't allow for that.

Our lips find one another's and we begin kissing again as the driver heads back to my hotel. Kissing him this time feels so much more than previously. With all the shit out of the way, all there is now is us and our strong feelings for one another. The longer we kiss, the harder his cock becomes beneath me. I've never wanted to be naked more so than I do right now.

"Saxon," I breathe against his lips, "I need you."

"Soon."

I grunt in defeat. He pulls back and stares at me, his gaze heated and carnal. It bores deep into my soul. "Elevator Girl, I want the first time I fuck you to be everything, I don't want a quickie in the back of a town car."

"Why are you so perfect?"

"Why are you?" he throws back at me.

From the front, the driver says, "We're here, sir."

Looking up, I see we are pulling in the hotel's driveway. Shuffling off his lap, I try and compose myself but I know my cheeks are flushed. The car comes to a stop and the concierge opens the door. Saxon climbs out, turns, and offers me his hand. Placing my palm in his, he helps me out. I duck my head back in. "Thank you," I tell the driver.

"My pleasure, Miss."

Standing back up, I look to Sax and my breath hitches in the back of my throat. Two days ago, I thought he was a player and the arrogant jerk in 7C. Now, I'm not sure exactly what our status is, but all I know is we need to be upstairs and naked. Now.

"I like what you're thinking, Elevator Girl."

"And just what am I thinking?"

He slides his arm around my waist, pulling me into his side. He leans down, his breath warming my already heated skin, he whispers, "You. Me. Naked."

My eyes widen. "How did you know?"

"Because it's exactly what I want right now."

"Then what are you waiting for?"

"Ab-so-fucking-lutely nothing."

He entwines our fingers and pulls me inside the hotel. We race across the lobby, with my heels click-clacking across the marble floor. The elevator is empty and waiting for us. It's like the gods know we're in a hurry. Stepping in, I press the button for my floor and before the doors have even closed, Saxon pushes me up against the back wall and covers my mouth with his. His hands glide down my body, my skin tingling at his touch. He tries to slide my hem up but this dress is figure hugging. He growls into my mouth and I giggle.

He pulls back and stares at me. "Something funny?"

"Nope," I say, shaking my head. Lifting my hand, I step my fingers up his chest. He grabs my hand in his.

"What are you doing?"

"Touching you."

He shakes his head. "Uh uh, Elevator Girl, I do all the touching."

"Have at it then," I tell him, pulling my hand from his. I slide my fingertips over my breasts and behind my neck. I fluff my hair before linking my fingers above my head.

"The things I'm going to do to you," he rasps, his voice deeper and huskier than usual.

"Have at it," I encourage him again, pushing my chest forward. His gaze drops to my breasts and then back up to my eyes.

The elevator dings, signaling our arrival at my floor. Just like at his parents' house earlier, he throws me over his shoulder and exits the metal car. "Which way?"

"Left," I instruct him but being upside down, I realize I'm wrong. "Right, I mean right."

He spins around and walks right. "Number?"

"The end one," I tell him, "1001."

He comes to a stop at my door. "Key?"

These one word questions are doing things to me that one word questions shouldn't.

"Put me down."

"Nope. Key."

Digging in my clutch, I pull out the room key card and hand it to him. He swipes it over the keypad and the lock clicks. He pushes the handle down and swings the door wide. Marching in, he stops and places me back on my feet; my body grazing down his until I land on the carpet.

We stare at one another. "Are you really here?" he asks, cupping my cheek in his palm.

"Yes, I'm here," I confirm, covering his hand with mine. "And I'm so sorry for not talking to you about all of this."

He presses his finger to my lips. "Shhhh, that's in the past. Right now, I want you naked and on that bed."

"So bossy," I reply, but his bossiness is a total turn-on. Stepping back from him, I lift my hand behind my back and grab the zipper. I gently tug and the dress opens at the back. Slipping my arms out, I shimmy the material over my hips, where it cascades to the floor in a silky heap, leaving me in nothing but my heels and G-string.

"Fuck me, you're beautiful." His eyes roam over me.

"As much as I love that tux on you, I'd much rather see what's underneath."

He nods and silently removes his suit jacket, then kicks off his shoes. Loosening the tie, he undoes the knot and begins to undo his buttons. My eyes are focused on his hands, watching each button pop open to reveal his muscular chest. Licking my lips, I lift my gaze back to his face and find him watching me intently.

When all the buttons are finally undone, I step to him and slide my palms across his pecs and drag his shirt down his arms, it floats to the floor landing on top of my dress. Dropping to my knees, I keep my eyes on his and I flip open the button on his trousers and lower the fly. Grabbing the waistband, I push his pants and briefs down his legs, freeing his cock.

The tip glistens. My mouth waters. My tongue darts out and I swipe it across the head, his salty taste dances on the tip of my tongue. He hisses and that sound vibrates through my body, causing my arousal to soak the material of my panties. I don't think I've ever been this turned on before.

With my eyes locked on his, I open my mouth and wrap my lips around his cock, sucking 'til the tip hits the back of my throat. My head bobs up and down. Gently I graze my teeth along his shaft, but he grips my head and pulls his length from my mouth. "As much as that is amazing, I need to taste you, Elevator Girl, before I fuck you. Now get onto the bed and show me your pussy."

I'm not normally one for dirty talk, but the words coming from Saxon are just what I want and need to hear right now. Standing to full height, I hook my fingers in my G-string and pull the material down my legs. Stepping out, I move backward toward the bed. My legs hit the mattress and I sit. Leaning down, I go to remove my heels.

"Shoes stay," he growls. The deep timbre of his voice sends shockwaves through my body. My clit thrums at the excitement of what's about to happen between us.

Nodding, I shuffle backward up the mattress. I'm trying to be sexy but I have no clue if I nail it, or if I look like a turtle on its back wriggling around. If I go by the look on Saxon's face right now, I definitely nailed it.

Lying back on the pillows, I stare up at a naked Saxon. My eyes ogle his body. Lifting my gaze to his, I open my legs as per his request. Feeling brazen, I slide my fingertip between the valley of my breasts, down my stomach, toward my pussy. My fingertip grazes my clit when Saxon reaches out and grips my wrist, halting me. He shakes his head and growls, "Mine."

Quicker than I've ever seen him move, he drops to his knees, grabs my ankles, pulls me to the edge of the bed, and has his head between my thighs. He licks me from taint to clit, his tongue flicking up and down my slit. If I thought my body was on fire before, I'm now a blazing inferno as he continues to lick, nibble, and suck me.

That feeling begins to develop low in my tummy. I don't think I've ever reached this point so quickly from oral before. Saxon is a freaking god with his tongue. He slips a finger in and plunges his digit in and out. His mouth paying close, very close, attention to my clit.

"Saxon," I moan, my voice deep and thready. He bites my clit and I explode. I come harder than I ever have before, soaking his face with my arousal. He sucks and licks every last drop from between my thighs.

Grabbing his head in my palms, I lift so he's looking at me. "Fuck me now, Saxon."

28

"FUCK ME NOW, SAXON." THE BEST FOUR WORDS I'VE ever heard in my life.

Crawling like a panther up her body, I hold myself up on my elbows and stare down at her. "With fucking pleasure." I lower my lips to hers and kiss her, then I remember protection. I jump up and she whines at the loss. "Protection," I tell her as I bend down and pick up my pants. Pulling out my wallet, I grab the condom and tear it open with my teeth.

She watches me as I sheath my cock. Stroking myself a few times, I gaze down at her. I can't believe we're about to do this. Six hours ago, I was in hell, and now, now I'm in fucking heaven. Elevator Girl is the most stunning woman in the world, but when she's naked and flushed after an orgasm, she's a fucking goddess.

She lifts her hand and beckons me forward with her finger. Resting my knee on the end of the bed, I lean down and crawl up her body. I situate myself between her thighs, leaning forward, I run my nose along her skin, causing goosebumps to appear.

Covering her body with mine, I hover over her, staring down into her gorgeous blue eyes. Lining my cock up at her entrance, I tease her before I push into her. Her eyes widen as I slide in. "Saxon," she moans when I'm fully inside her.

With our eyes locked on one another, I thrust in and out of her. Her walls clench my shaft. Hugging my cock tightly before I slide back out.

In.

Out.

In.

Out.

I thrust over and over. My balls begin to tingle but I refuse to come until she does.

"I'm close," she mewls.

Wrapping her arms around my neck, she pulls me down and slams her lips to mine. The slight change in angle sets her off and she screams her release into my mouth. She's still coming down from her high when I find my release. Grunting and groaning, spilling my seed into the condom.

"Wow," she mumbles against my lips.

"Wow, indeed," I reply.

Climbing off the bed, I remove the condom and drop it to the carpet. Climbing back onto the bed, Simone snuggles into my side. Her head resting on my chest. Wrapping my arms around her, I blissfully drift off to sleep with Elevator Girl in my arms. Happier than I've ever been.

Well, until I wake the next morning with Simone's lips gloriously wrapped around my cock. FYI, this is my new favourite way to wake up.

After coming down her throat, she slides back next to me and stares up at me. "Morning," she sheepishly whispers.

Lowering my head, I go to kiss her but she ducks and hides her pretty face.

"Why you hiding from me?"

"I have morning and spunk breath," she says, lifting her head so I can see her eyes but not her mouth.

"I don't care about morning or spunk breath," I honestly tell her, and it's true. I don't care about that; all I care about right now is kissing her and then fucking her. She's unleashed something within me and I need to be inside her all the time now. Hence why we got little sleep last night. Every time she moved and touched me, it sparked my dick to life and I had to fuck her.

I'm addicted to her and she's the best addiction to have.

"I do," she protests, pushing off my chest and wriggling away from me, but my reflexes are quicker and I flip her to her back.

"Kiss me," I demand.

"No!" she protests and turns her head to the side.

"Elevator Girl," I sternly say, "kiss me now or else."

"Or else what?" she sasses.

"Or else..."

"Nothing, you got nothing. Now get off me. Let me brush my teeth, and THEN I'll kiss you for the rest of the day."

The idea of kissing her all day long is tempting but I received a text earlier from Soraya, and we've been summoned for brunch at the haunted house on the hill. "Fine...but then we need to jump in the shower and get ready for brunch."

"How sweet, you're taking me to brunch."

"You won't be thanking me later."

"How come?"

"We've been summoned to the haunted house on the hill."

"If you mean the gorgeous McMansion we were at last night, then I don't mind at all."

"Really?" I ask, shocked. "You're happy to do brunch with the rents?"

"I'd much rather do you, but you and I have plenty of time for that. You're only here 'til Monday and you need to see your parents."

"But—"

She presses her fingers to her lips. "No buts. I understand they aren't the best parents in the world but they're your parents. I would give anything to be able to have brunch with my mom."

"You really are something."

"A good something?"

"A very good something. Maybe we should shower together to be water savvy and all that shit."

"Deal."

Simone brushes her teeth and I start the shower. Our shower takes a little longer than it should, and I'm not sure how much water we saved, but as soon as my lips touched hers, nothing else mattered except bringing pleasure to my woman.

29

SIMONE

...a few months later

"You ready, Doctor?"

"I feel like I want to throw up," I tell him.

"Babe, you've got this. You were born to be a doctor and today, you're going to rock." Today is the first day of my residency and I'm so nervous. I thought the interview and wait were nerve-wracking, but today I'm a mess.

Dad called me earlier to wish me luck. He and Maree were heading out for a celebratory brunch in my honor.

"You have to say that."

"I'm only stating the truth."

"No, you just want kisses and blow jobs so you're saying nice things to me."

"Well, I do love your kisses and blow jobs but I assure you, this is not a suck-up. Babe, you've got this. You beat out a hundred and fifty other people. You earned this. You."

"I love you, Just Saxon," I tell him, placing a kiss on the tip of his nose. He has become my everything and I'm so happy that it was just a misunderstanding all those months ago.

"And I love you, too, Elevator Girl. Now go and be the kick-ass doctor that I know you are and tonight, tonight we'll celebrate in style."

"Blow jobs and kisses?" I ask, raising my eyebrows suggestively.

"Not what I had in mind but I'm sure I can work blow jobs and kisses into the evening's festivities.

He steps to me and presses his lips to mine. I love kissing him but most of all, I love who I am with him. Breaking the kiss, I grab my bag and I exit my apartment.

Pressing the call button, I wait for the elevator, ready to embark on the next adventure of my career. I'm nervous but most of all, I'm happy. I look toward 7C and grin, who knew that I would find love and happiness with the jerk in 7C.

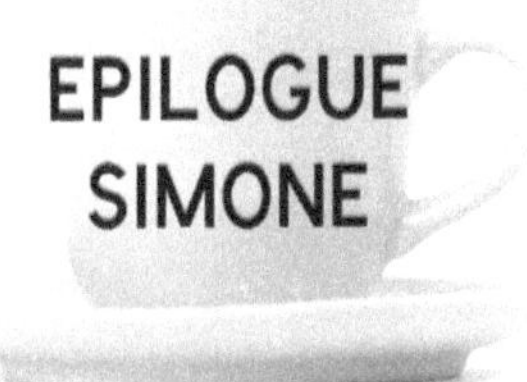

...four years later

“Dr. Mitchel, you’re needed in three.”

“Thanks, Sue,” I tell the head nurse. I still get a rush when people refer to me as doctor. Dad and Sax have been doing it since forever but when strangers or my colleagues do it, it gives me a rush.

With a smile on my face, I head toward three. Looking at the clock, I see that I have fifteen minutes left on my shift. This is my last shift as part of the residency program. When I walk through these doors tomorrow, I’m on my own. I’m officially, officially a doctor.

I was lucky to snag an attending position here at the hospital, so it’s an easy transition for me. It’s hard to believe that after twelve years of school, four years of college, four years of medical school, and my residency, I'm officially a doctor. Sure, I was technically one when I received my medical license but the training is ongoing.

Pulling back the curtain to three, I pull it closed behind me and as I turn around, I give my spiel. "Hi, I'm Dr. Mitchel, what can I do for you toda—" When I look up, I see Saxon sitting on the edge of the bed in a tux looking sexy AF. "Sax, what are you doing here?"

"I needed to see a doctor."

"And what could possibly be wrong?"

"It's my heart," he says, lifting his hand and pressing it to his chest. "It's been beating erratically all day long."

"Any other symptoms?" I question, stepping over to him. I place my fingers on his wrist to count his pulse. "It's a little fast," I tell him, starting to get anxious that something really is wrong.

Placing my stethoscope in my ears, I lift the bell and rest it on his chest. "It all sounds okay." I rest my palm on his forehead and notice he's clammy. "You're hot."

"I know," he teasingly says.

"Sax, this is serious," I reprimand him.

"I'm sure it's nothing serious," he nonchalantly says with a shrug, his blasé attitude right now is pissing me off.

"I'm going to order an ECG and blood work." I turn to walk out and order the tests.

"Stop," he loudly yells. He grips onto my wrist, halting me, and then I feel a tug as he drops to the ground behind me.

"Saxon," I screech, but when I turn around, I see he's down on one knee. In the hand not holding my wrist is a ring—Mom's engagement ring.

He lets go of my wrist and grabs my left hand. "Simone Meredith Mitchel, Elevator Girl, and kick-ass doctor. You are my everything and I want you to be my everything forever. Will you do me the absolute honor of becoming my wife?"

Staring down at Sax on bended knee, I'm speechless. I've been so focused on work and life that I never knew this was on his radar. It's been on my mind, hello, I'm a girl and I've been dreaming of this ever since I got Bridal Barbie when I was five.

Sweat lines his forehead. His hazel eyes stare up at me, waiting for my answer. My head begins to nod up and down.

A smile appears on his face. "Is that a yes nod?"

My nodding increases. "It's a yes nod. A thousand times yes."

He slips Mom's ring on to my finger and it fits perfectly. He must sense my confusion. "I had it resized to fit after I asked your dad."

"You asked Dad?"

"You bet he did." I hear Dad's voice from behind the curtain. My eyes widen and my mouth drops open. The surprises just keep coming today. Sax rises to his feet and pulls back the curtain. Standing before me is Dad, Maree, Nadine, Marshall, Eloise, their kids, Grayson, Soraya, their little girl, and the rest of my work colleagues.

"What are you all doing here?" I ask.

"DUH, celebrating your engagement," Nadine teases, a smile graces her face.

Turning to my fiancé, I gaze at him. "You did all of this?"

He nods.

"For me?"

Again he nods.

"Elevator Girl, I would do anything for you."

"Anything?" I suggestively raise my eyebrows at him, alluding to the little game we like to play together. You see, we like to play the 'he's my arrogant jerk neighbor playing loud music and when I confront him…' well, you can guess what happens next. **WINK WINK**

"Definitely anything," he says. Stepping to him, I grip his cheeks in my palms, and for a few beats I stare at Mom's ring on my finger before I press my lips to his. I love kissing Saxon but now that we're engaged, it feels so much more.

Everyone around us whistles and then congratulations are passed around. Taking a moment, I stop and stare at my fiancé. "Just Sax, are you sure everything is okay? You were clammy and your heart rate WAS elevated."

"I was nervous because of asking you to marry me."

"Ohh, yeah, that," I say. Lifting my hand, I gaze down at Mom's ring.

"Are you okay that I used your mom's and didn't get you one of your own?"

Nodding, I find my smile widening. "So, so happy. I wish you could have met her."

"Me too, babe. Me too. Now, how about we take this to Nobel's for the celebrations to continue?"

"I still have to finish my shift an—"

"No you don't," my boss says, "go and celebrate your engagement and officially becoming an attending."

"Are you sure?"

"I'm sure. No one puts in more hours or effort than you, Dr. Mitchel, now go...or I'll fire you before you even start."

"Thank you," I tell my boss. Looking to Sax, I instruct, "Give me a sec to go change and then we can head to Nobel's."

Just as I say this, Nadine appears with a black garment bag. "You'll need this." She links her arm with mine and leads me to the staffroom. I quickly change into the emerald green halter dress that Sax arranged for me.

After touching up my make up, we head back out to meet my fiancé and family.

As a group, we all make our way to Nobel's to celebrate.

Leaning against the bar, I look around at all those I love most in the world and smile. I really am a lucky lady. Saxon looks over to me and just like that first day we met near the elevators, my heart stops beating. Saxon Nobel, the guy in 7C, is my everything and I cannot wait to marry him.

EPILOGUE
SAXON

"Yo, jerk," a sexy as hell woman growls when I open the door. "Mind not playing your music so loud?"

"Huh," I ask, playing dumb.

"Your music, every morning since you moved in it's been dance party central in 7C."

Staring at the feisty woman before me, in nothing but a sexy midnight blue negligée, my cock twitches. "Yo, jerk, my eyes are up here."

Lifting my gaze from her body, I stare into the most amazing set of blue eyes I have ever seen and then I realize it's her. "Elevator Girl?"

Her eyes widen. "You?" she growls again, and fuck me, hearing her growl is such a turn on. "How? What?"

"Just Saxon," I say, offering my hand. "The guy in 7C."

"Elevator Girl, the girl in 7B." She places her hand in mine and like we always do when we play this game, I pull her into my arms and slam my lips against hers. She grips my cheeks in her palms and deepens our kiss.

Sliding my hand around her waist and down to her ass, I tap and she jumps into my arms. Wrapping her legs around me, I kick the door closed, and press her back into the wood.

Gyrating my hips, my cock grinds against her center. She moans into the kiss. "Fuck me, Saxon," she purrs against my lips.

Lowering my hand from her ass, I slide it up her thigh. Brushing past her pussy, I make quick work of lowering my fly and freeing my cock. Pressing my length into her, she circles her hips. "Please," she begs.

"I love it when you beg, Elevator Girl."

"Please, Sax, fuck me now."

"With pleasure." Pulling her panties to the side, I thrust my hips and press my length inside her. We both moan as her pussy hugs my cock as I slide in and out of her tight wet channel.

My eyes are locked on her gorgeous face. Her eyes are closed. Her cheeks and neck are flushed in my favorite shade of aroused pink. She bites her plump bottom lip. "Fuuuuck, I love when you do that."

She opens her eyes and we gaze intently at one another as I continue to thrust in and out of her. "I'm close," she mewls.

Winking at her, I grip her hips in my hands and I pound into her harder. Her head bumping the door with my frenzied thrusts. "Saaaaaxon," she screams, as she crashes over the orgasmic cliff. Her pussy pulsates around my cock and I explode inside her. Fucking her bare is so much more than I ever thought it would be.

When we made the decision to do that we both got tested to make sure we were clean. She was already on the implant thingy so we were covered birth control wise. The first time we did it bare, it was quick, way too quick for a grown man, but it was so much more intense.

Resting my forehead against her, I'm panting heavily. Spinning around, I slide down the door with her in my lap. "I love this game of ours."

"Me too," she breathlessly replies, snuggling into me. "I cannot wait to marry you and have 'fake fight make-up sex' with you whenever I want." She places a kiss to my chest and then stares at me.

"Yes, 'Fake fight make-up sex' is a favorite of mine too, Elevator Girl, but I think 'husband and wife I'll love you to the day I die sex' will be so much better."

"I like the sound of that but before we get to that, how about 'Fiancée, I love you, fuck me now sex?'"

"I can get on board with that."

She leans forward and presses her lips to mine. Even though I've just come, and I'm still inside her, my cock hardens again.

"Again? Right now? Really?" she questions.

"Hey, I have no control over my dick when it's near your cu—pussy." She eyes me, she hates the 'c' word and if I'm honest, I sometime say it just to taunt her. After all, pissing her off is one of the reasons she loves me so much.

Much to my disgust, she stands up and steps back. With her eyes locked on me, she lifts her hands, grabs the hem of her nightie, and lifts it over her head. Leaving her in nothing but her black lacy panties.

Slipping her hands into the waistband of her panties, she rolls them down her thighs. She stands upright and begins to walk backward, beckoning her to me with her finger. Rising to my feet, I grab my shirt by the collar at the back, and lift it over my head, dropping it to the floor beside me.

"Why is it so sexy when a guy does that?"

"This is even sexier," I growl. Flipping the button on my slacks, I lower the zipper and remove my pants, leaving me in just my briefs.

"I've seen sexier," she teases.

Palming my dick through my briefs, I grab the waistband of my underwear and push them down. Kicking them off, I stroke my dick with my eyes locked on hers. With her hand between her thighs, she whimpers.

We stand in the living room, rubbing ourselves.

"I love you, soon-to-be Mrs. Nobel."

"And I love you to the moon and back, Just Saxon."

She removes her hand from between her legs and beckons me to her. Stalking over to her, I pick her up, and march into our bedroom. Throwing her onto the bed, she bounces and squeals before shimming up the mattress. She beckons me forward, and who am I to deny my naked and horny fiancée?

Climbing onto the bed, ever so slowly, I slide up her delectable body Hovering above her, I stare down at her. She lifts her left hand and cups my cheek, with my eyes locked on her, I slide inside her. Slowly we rock back and forth with our eyes steadfastly locked on one another. Simone flips me onto my back and rolls on top of me. She straddles me and slides down my dick, riding me slowly, and together we come. Groaning each other's name as the pleasure envelops us.

After showering, we climb back into bed and snuggle. Simone is exhausted and immediately drifts off to sleep, but for some reason, sleep eludes me. Kissing her on the forehead, I gaze down at my beautiful sleeping fiancée and smile. The girl in 7B is my everything and I cannot wait to marry her.

THE END!!!!!!!

ACKNOWLEDGEMENTS

Thank you to **my family; Troy, Piper** and **Kade.** You three are my rocks, my loveable pains in the butt who push me to be the best. You are my everything. Love you all to the moon and back XoXoX

My beta babes; **Alana, Andi, Stef** and **Tara;** thank you ladies once again for reading my book baby and giving me your opinions and feedback. You gals are rock stars and I would be lost without you.

My editor, **Karen**, from **Barren Acres Editing;** I'm running out of things to say. You're not only my editor, but you're also a great friend; why do you live so far away? Thank you, once again for helping me turn my book baby from a pile of crap into a beautiful book baby and I will always be thankful for THAT!!!

My cover designer, **Kristie** from **Vanilla Lily Designs**. As soon as I saw this cover, I fell in love and I just had to have it and then this project came along and I think it was fate. Thank you for always putting up with my last minute changes and doing it with a smile.
I also need to thank **Amanda** from **Amanda Walker**

Design & PA for the stunning alternate. Like the original, as soon as I saw it, I had to have it. It screamed "Dana this is perfect for Saxon and Simone" and I couldn't agree more.

To **my readers**, thank you for the kind words that you message me with each release. 9 out of 10 times, these arrive just when I need a pick me up and they always do. From the bottom of my heart, thank you for supporting me and my books.

Cheers,
Dana Xo

ALSO BY DL GALLIE

STAND ALONES

Antecedent

Doc Steel

Oops

Off the Books

Fractured:A driven world novel

Deck...the Balls

Secrets and Sunrises

Always in the Cards

Out of Nowhere

Before the Ashes

After the Ashes

Love Me Like You Do

Never Let Me Go

Seven Nights

Seven Kisses

PUCKING NOVELS

I Pucking Hate That I Love You

A Pucking Good Christmas

...and a few pucking more

FALLING NOVELS

These men make it hard not to fall for them

Falling for Dr. Kelly

Falling for Dr. Knight

Falling for Agent Cox

Falling for Agent Cruz

Falling: The Complete Collection

LORDS OF CRESTWOOD PREP

Co-write with Tara Lee

Thatcher

Reign

Hendrix

Saint

THE UNEXPECTED SERIES

When it comes to love, expect the unexpected

The Unexpected Gift

The Unexpected Letter

The Unexpected Package

The Unexpected Connection

The Unexpected series: The Complete Collection

THE CASTAWAY GROVE COLLECTION

Love has arrived in the Grove

Oasis

Unequivocal Love

Five Words

Broken Rules

...and a few more to come.

The Castaway Grove Collection, Vol 1

THE LIQUOR CABINET SERIES

Liquor has never been so disturbingly saucy

Malt Me (Book 1)

Tequila Healing (Book 2)

Wine Not (Book 3)

The Final Shot (Book 4)

The Liquor Cabinet: Series boxset

All of these books are available on Amazon.

FACEBOOK ~ INSTAGRAM ~ BOOKBUB

GOODREADS ~ WEBSITE

dlgallieauthor@outlook.com

Sign up to my newsletter

ABOUT THE AUTHOR

DL Gallie is from Queensland, Australia, but she's lived in many different places all over the world, including the UK and Canada. She currently resides in Central Queensland with her husband and two munchkins. She and her husband have been together since she was sixteen, and although they drive each other crazy at times, she couldn't imagine her life without him.

Shortly after her son was born, DL began reading again. With encouragement from her husband, she picked up the pen and started writing, and now the voices in her head won't shut up.

DL enjoys listening to music, drinking white wine in the summer, red wine in the winter, and beer all year round. She's also never been known to turn down a cocktail, especially a margarita.

www.ingramcontent.com/pod-product-compliance
Lightning Source LLC
Chambersburg PA
CBHW020330030826
48979CB00021B/510

* 9 7 8 0 6 4 5 8 1 2 1 9 0 *